The Segovia Chronicles

Other books by Paul Ruffin:

The Man Who Would Be God (stories)
Islands, Women, and God (stories)
Jesus in the Mist (stories)
Pompeii Man (novel)
Castle in the Gloom (novel)
Here's to Noah, Bless His Ark (essays)
Lighting the Furnace Pilot (poetry)
Circling (poetry)
The Book of Boys and Girls (poetry)

The Segovia Chronicles

For Kevin,
with gratitude

Paul

Paul Ruffin

Louisiana Literature Press
Hammond, Louisiana

FIRST EDITION, 2006

Requests for permission to reproduce material from this work should be
sent to:

Permissions
Louisiana Literature Press
Southeastern Louisiana University
Box 10792
Hammond, LA 70402

Acknowledgments:

I wish to thank the following journals, in which several of these
pieces appeared: *The Distillery, Meridian, Pembroke Magazine,
Southwestern American Literature*

Library of Congress Cataloging-in-Publication Data

Ruffin, Paul.
 The Segovia chronicles / Paul Ruffin. -- 1st ed.
  p. cm.
 ISBN-13: 978-0-945083-17-7 (cloth)
 ISBN-10: 0-945083-17-3 (cloth : alk. paper)
 ISBN-13: 978-0-945083-18-4 (pbk.)
 ISBN-10: 0-945083-18-1 (pbk. : alk. paper)
 1. Texas--Social life and customs--Fiction. I. Title.
 PS3568.U362S44 2006
 813'.54--dc22
                          2006032233

This book is dedicated

to Bob and Shirley Winship,

whose friendship I shall

forever cherish.

Table of Contents

From the Front Porch

The People and the Land

Returning to Segovia: a Story

Foreword

I may honestly say that my maturation as a writer was not fully realized until, by a stroke of luck that I still do not understand, I came into the presence of Bob Winship.

Our history is a long one, so I will not waste the space here to chronicle it. I will say only that sometime nearly twenty years ago, I made my first trip to the Rockpile Ranch, Bob's family place, and I have been going back several times a year since.

Bob and Shirley Winship are a glorious couple, perfectly matched, and they are people of family, of food, and of fun. What else is there that matters? Smart? Oh yeah. Hardworking? Yessir. Independent? You bet. They are everything one might hope to find in a pair of friends.

Now, the Rockpile is, by Texas standards, a fairly small ranch—just a section, something over 600 acres. But it has everything: a stretch of flatland oat patches bounded by strips of mesquite, a loop of pristine river, and three high hills swarming with cedars and oak and a variety of animals that I will not presume to list. It is an Edenic spot, and I have never been there when I didn't feel that I was leaving my burdens at the gate.

What I knew of West Texas when my wife and I moved out here was all I remembered from a trip from El Paso across to Beaumont on the way back from Califonia. It looked dry and desolate, with breathtaking mountains and panoramic river valleys. But we were hell-bent to get back to Mississippi, so we stopped only once or twice during that twenty-something-hour mad dash across the state in a VW Beetle, if you could call it a dash. It was definitely *mad*.

After moving out to Texas to take a job at Sam Houston State University, I made occasional trips over as far west as San

Antonio and south to Brownsville, but it was only after Winship came into my life and I inherited a lifetime invitation to visit the Rockpile whenever I wished that I came to know that land and its people.

Soon West Texas became a part of my writing, especially the area of Segovia, the little river-valley community that once had a post office and store and school but now is just ranchland. The old post office building remains, as does the school, but one is ruins, the other a residence. And there's the truck stop up on the interstate.

I have set a number of stories out there and countless essays. This book is a compilation of some of those pieces. Some of the tales here are true, some are not; some of the people are real, some are not. It doesn't really matter whether they are true and real, so long as I convince you through my writing that they are or could be.

The Rockpile Ranch, then, is a place I call home, and I always will. Sometimes when the world is too much with me, I will kick back and imagine myself in one of the draws or up in the hills, watching the sun drop over a far cliff or spill its early light into the valley, lying on my back up in the rocks at night with my son watching for satellites in that vast empyrean of crystal space, drinking Ste. Genevieve wine and rocking with Bob and Shirley in the breezeway between the old and new wings of the ranchhouse watching evening settle, taking a deep slug of that iron-tinged water from the well, or relishing one of Shirley's late-morning breakfast casseroles. That river valley and ranch have been one of the greatest inspirations of my life, and I suspect that they will continue to be for a very long time to come. I hope that you will enjoy this journey to that magic country. —*Paul Ruffin*

Segovio Prologue

Down in south-central Texas there is a place where two river valleys come together as the smaller of the rivers flows north into the other. This happens between the 99th and 100th meridians as the Llano River makes its pristine-clear way eastward to the Gulf.

Where the valleys join, a bluff looks into the morning sun like a great gothic gargoyle. Like the rusty prow of a wrecked ship it towers out of a tangle of cedar, mesquite, boulders and cactus as if still aiming at an unfulfilled promise: something it refuses to forget.

This is Cloud Point, and a Texas Historical marker just below on a blacktop called FM 2169 gives the reason for such an attitude. A hundred years ago several roads and highways coalesced here. And the spot was known far and wide as the mid-point between Florida and California, across the continental United States.

South of Cloud Point five miles, in the valley of the Johnson Fork, lies the hamlet of Segovia, Texas, the modern claimant to the throne which Cloud Point consummated and lost: for here crossing FM 2169 east to west is mighty Interstate Ten, the giant transcontinental roadway from Jacksonville, Florida, to Los Angeles, California. And if you get a map of Dwight Eisenhower's infrastructure as big as an auditorium, and measure the curves and corners of I-10 with a hundred-foot tape, you will find Segovia exactly in the middle. Exactly. Heavy duty, indeed, for a village so small.

Segovia was not always so small. Now the midpoint is marked only by a truckstop and truckstop restaurant, but in ages past the community had a post office, a schoolhouse, a church, and a racetrack. The racetrack came first and the church last, however: and herein our plot thickens. This fact tells you something about the people who lived here and the people who still live here. There is a reason they are different.

Texas historian Walter Prescott Webb had a great deal to say about the story of this location, by way of explanation. According to Webb—and others—the 1800's colonizing east-to-west progression at this latitude bogged down just beyond the 98th meridian because the settlers ran out of straight posts for their fences and water for irrigation. Then the Civil War intervened, during which time the Comanches and Kiowas wreaked much havoc in the area because most protecting males were away at the war. Then, in 1874, two things happened independently that made a great difference in the efficacy of westward expansion: The windmill was invented, and barbed wire was invented. Water and fencing material, all at once.

So almost immediately the settlers were all the way to the Left Coast. But two things about the renascence of pilgrimage were important: To this point the movement had been farmers, now it was ranchers.

Webb says further that whereas any place in the continental United States had fifteen years of frontier on the average, the residents of the 98th, 99th, and 100th meridians had fifty years of frontier. As a matter of fact, it has been said by others that 150 years after the founding of San Antonio it was still possible to get scalped on the edge of town.

But the history of man in this place is miniscule compared to the history of the land. Stand on tiptoe above I-10 outside the Segovia Truckstop Restaurant and look in all directions and you can count eleven cliffs—Cloud Point the farthest to the north, and to the south a similar distance, one above old Joy Settlement, where the racetrack used to be.

In all these cliffs are fossilized corkscrews and bivalves harking back five hundred million years to when the whole area was a seabed. And this is limestone country: All the bluffs were made by the Johnson Fork eons before it was so named, as it meandered back and forth across the valley after the sea had gone. How long after? Dinosaur tracks dating back a hundred and ten million years to the Cretaceous Period can be seen in river rock at Joy Colony. Mention this carving of cliffs to a local here and he will smirk and say, "I don't know, man. I've been here fifty years and I never saw anything like that!"

So many cliffs in fact exist that the name of the place used to be Cliffdale. Then Teddy Roosevelt bivouacked in the area in 1898 and took a couple of local residents with him to Spain. When they returned they renamed the place. You guessed it: Segovia. One wonders what it was that reminded this land of Sam Maverick and cattle drives of that sophisticated city of Spain . . . .

So the newly-named village found itself already in a spectacular pastoral phase: As late in its post-frontier history as 1938, both sides of the Johnson Fork all the way from the famous stage stop Joy Colony to the main Llano were nothing but truck farms.

Squash, beans, peas, tomatoes, potatoes, okra, onions, cucumbers, carrots—and lots and lots of corn—occupied row upon row of space by the river as big single-cylinder Krueger-Atlas engines hammered the clear air and pumped water into the rows out of the Johnson Fork. Probably also in 1938, or thereabouts, the county had, by one-third, more people than it had had before, or has had since. Year by year, from 1938 until now, the farm phase has passed. Slowly. Completely.

The county is Kimble, and Segovia tends to the southeast. Kimble County has spectacular beauty: It is known as one of the showplaces of Texas. Hill Country, it is called, and the county has more miles of running water than any other county in Texas. Not lakes: mountain streams. Also the largest herd of whitetail deer in the world centers exactly here, and for a reason.

That reason is cover. Kimble is a good place to hide. This fact has never gone ignored: Badmen and outlaws have hid out here since the Texas Rangers stopped fighting Comanches and found more and more of their time taken up with white men. As a matter of fact, gunfighter John Wesley Hardin was married in Kimble. Sam Bass allegedly spent some time here; and it is a proven fact that Bonnie and Clyde lived here much of the time. They had just left Kimble County, Texas, when they met their demise by gunfire in Louisiana.

J. Frank Dobie, in his history of the Texas Rangers, makes a funny. The Rangers had rounded up a whole corral full of Kimble County badmen, according to Dobie, and went looking for twelve honest men with which to form a jury for a trial.

Twelve honest men could not be found, says Dobie. So the badmen had to be released. *Habeas corpus*, or some such. So now in the present day we have locals who come to eat the famous Segovia Restaurant breakfast who have in their heritage fifty years of frontier instead of the national norm of fifteen. Independent? Stubborn? Sovereign? You got it.

And they rub shoulders at the tables with modern-day truckers from Jacksonville and Los Angeles and all points between. Segovia Truck Stop is a microcosm of alloy, blend, and medley in human affairs today, perhaps unique in the world in terms of vigor and spontaneity, mixing of the old and the new.

But there are other places—a lot of them—where the past mixes with the present, every day. What of the future, to complete the triad?

Long-time rumor has it that westbound from Segovia Truck Stop on I-10 a scant two miles away, the Alcan Highway is being built—extended might be a better term—from Anchorage, Alaska, to Tierra del Fuego, at the southern tip of South America. It will cross I-10 near enough for such union to be called Segovia Crossing, maybe. How's that for future?

Or, perhaps more appropriately, how's that for scope?

—*Robert Winship*

The Segovia Chronicles

From the Front Porch

Bowhunters, Dogs, and Women

"One hell of a bunch," Mr. Pate is saying as he works on a chew of something dark whose juice trickles down the corners of his mouth.

Mr. Pate lives a few miles from Junction, Texas, a long mile or so down Old Segovia Road from friend Bob Winship's Rockpile Ranch. Winship and I have just walked that mile, and we're sitting on his stone-floored porch having a beer. So in the redolent evening air the old man reaches and fishes another Ziegenbock from the ice-filled galvanized bucket, his voice gravelly as the bottom of the Johnson Fork. He knocks the beer down in three chugs. He is telling us about the bowhunters who come out to his place to hunt deer, whitetails and exotics. Bob is studying an enormous catfish skull that must have weighed forty pounds on the hoof, as they say out here, running his fingers over the delicate lines of lips and eye sockets. Bleached almost white by the sun, it has a wide bony grin. Off through the pecan orchard I can see the surface of the Johnson fork of the Llano twinkling in late afternoon sun.

"Come out of a hole in the river down there," the old man says, gesturing toward the sheen of water. "One of my boys caught it on a trotline." I nod. I grew up in Mississippi—I know about trotlines and catfish.

"So what're you saying about bowhunters?" Winship has brought me here to listen to the old man talk about them.

"I'm sayin' that by and large—and let me clean this up for you since you might not like bad language, bein' a perfesser and all—they ain't got horse shit for brains." He spits into his coffee can and says to Winship, "Go get some more beer out of the icebox, Bobby, put'm in that bucket."

"Enlighten him," Winship encourages. "He's led a sheltered life. I'll get the beer."

Mr. Pate rolls his rheumy eyes toward Bob, then toward the river. "First off, ever damned one of'm's got too much—" He pauses a long time, his head to the side like some sort of wise bird, and raises his voice toward Bob, who's off in the kitchen. "Hey, Winship, you went to medical school. What's the male juice called? The word *high-test*, like in gasoline, is rattlin' around in my mind, but it ain't that."

"Close," Bob says, coming back onto the porch with three ZiegenBocks gripped at the necks in each hand like dead ducks. "What you're fishing for is *testosterone*. It's a hormone."

The old man takes his Ziegy and snickers. "I remember a joke that you boys might like. One scientist asks the other does he know how to make a hormone, and—"

"Ruffin already knows that one, Mr. Pate. I told him. Matter of fact, I told *you* that joke. He wants to hear about bowhunters."

"Right." The old man shifts in his seat, swigs deep, and levels his eyes at me. "To start with, ever one of'm's got testyrone poisonin'. That's the main thang makes'm want to hunt with bows anyhow. It's like cuckleburrs in they blood. Got hair on their arms and back and chest, shoulders, runs together on their neck, like a pelt. Gotta trim up ever eight hours. They get them Dr. Pepper shadders."

"Like a five-o'clock shadow, Ruffin, only ten, two, and four," Winship explains. "It's another one of his jokes."

"Them ol' boys don't feel right totin' a gun. Sissy stuff. You know, they ain't nothin' but cavemen that managed to get born too late."

"Yow," I say, looking at Bob. "Mr. Pate's down on the boys with the bows."

"All I know's I got six that comes out here reglar to hunt, and there ain't one of'm the dogs like. And that to me is the biggest sign they is. Take Ralph there." He motions to an old rangy red hound sprawled out in front of us. "He ain't got the energy to lift his head to take a drink of water. Eats with his face flat down on that rock floor. Lay his food in front of him and he laps it without ever liftin' his head. A herd of buffalo couldn't stir him if they was to come across the porch, even if they stepped on him." The dog rolls one eye toward Mr. Pate, grunts, and twitches his tail. "Smart, though. He knows I'm talkin' about him."

"You used his name," Bob says.

"He knowed anyway," the old man grumbles. "Point is, you let a bowhunter pull up out there— Ralph'll know it's a bowhunter when he turns off the road—and that dog'll bounce to his feet like a barefooted teenager done stepped on a lit cigarette and start raisin' absolute and holy hell about it. Hackles up like a boar hawg, lips pulled all the way back to the hurtin' point, growlin'. Then ol' Judge'll join in. He's bad news all the way around—part Rott, part German Shepherd, part a bunch of other thangs, a Brunsick—so I keep him chained out back, but twice he's broke aloose to get at a bowhunter—"

"Brunsick? I've never heard of a Brunsick." I look over at Winship.

"He means Brunswick, as in Brunswick Stew."

"At's right," Mr. Pate affirms. "Got a little bit of everthang in'm."

"OK."

"At any rate, when a bowhunter shows up, I have to beat the two of'm back, lock'm up in the house. Otherwise, they would't even let one of'm get outta the truck. And I got to keep'm in the house or chained the whole time them guys is out here." He leans back and nods, working on his beer. "Dogs know. Dogs got'm figgered. Dogs and women and kids—they know stuff like that."

"They probably smell the testosterone—the dogs, I mean," Bob suggests.

"You rekkin, huh? I figger it's because they know that a bowhunter would just as soon shoot and eat a dog as a deer. Skin'm out and cut their heads and feet and hickeys off and who could tell? Ain't nothin' safe out here when they around. I remember one time—"

"Mr. Pate," Winship breaks in. He has to keep the old man oriented.

I ask, "Why do they keep coming here if they know the kind of welcome they're going to get?"

"Why? For one thang, I bet all dogs treat'm like that, so they figger all dogs is the same and Ralph and Judge ain't any different. But the real reason is because I got big herds of axis and sika and fallow, aoudads, mouflons, plus great big whitetail. Turkeys, hawgs. You name it, it roams these hills and bottoms. Even got them big yeller cats. You know, the Y-O Ranch ain't but six miles that direction."

He points off toward the hills. "They the ones brought in all them zotics back in the forties that excaped to everwhere. The bowhunters get to take home meat is how come they keep on. Well now, they might not take home meat, but they sure God get to slang arrers at some. You can get over a whole lot of mean dogs if you know you gon' get in some good shootin'."

"OK. Let me take another approach. If you and the dogs don't like bowhunters, why do you let them hunt here?"

He looks wisely over at me and shoots a vile-looking stream into his can. "You take their money and mix it up with a handful from rifle hunters or a collection at church and you can't tell the difference. That's how come. Their money banks like any other."

Bob lays the grinning catfish skull down next to the dog, who slowly opens one eye halfway, then closes it. "Mr. Pate, tell the Doc"—that's what Winship calls me sometimes, the Doc—"the other reason why these guys like to use bows."

The old man leans forward in his chair and stares at him. "Hell, Bobby, they's a lot more'n one other."

"I mean what you told me about women."

Mr. Pate nods. "Oh. All right. Yeah. Another reason these guys like a bow is that a woman can't use one. Or at least I never seen one could pull a big bow all the way back. They might be able to work them little target bows, but not no big huntin' bow. They go red in the face tryin', but I ain't seen one yet could get one all the way back. I wouldn't want to cross no gal that could. It's the only weapon a woman can't use like a man."

Winship explains: "Takes too much upper-body strength."

"Nossir, a woman ain't built for no bow. They can handle a rifle or pistol, knife, screwdriver, wrench, lawnmower, airplane, boat, truck, whatever. They can snatch a lanyard on a howitzer. And Lord knows what they can just in general do to *men*. But they can't use no bow."

"Well sir, that's not exactly true, is it?" Winship breaks in It's obvious to me that he's urging Mr. Pate in a direction. I know Bob.

The old man glances down at the grinning

skull and cackles. "Not exactly, no. Rekkin I ought to tell the perfesser about—."

"Oh yeah," Winship says, getting up and collecting our empties. "Lay it on him."

I settle back to listen.

"Well, I seen her drive up to the cabins while he was off at the truck stop with a gal named Ludy for breakfast. The bowhunter, a life-insurance salesman out of Houston, had done spent the night with her up in one of the hunters' cabins, and I guess the little lady back home sensed somethin' was goin' on—I mean, women always do, like Ralph and Judge knows the sound of a bowhunter arrivin'–"

"They smell the testosterone," Winship says. "The women, not the dogs. I mean, the dogs do too, of course." He has the skull to his face, squinting from the back side through the eye holes. It's eerie looking, like some kind of mask a savage might put on to do a victory dance.

"Whatever, they *know*. You can write that down. My momma hated bowhunters."

"She passed away a few years back," Bob explains, lowering the skull.

"She did. Had the sugar di-beetees, then the cancer. Died the same day them people burned up in Waco. I believe them chilren burnin' up might have helped push her thoo to the other side. Point is, she could not stand bowhunters. Had a sixth or seventh sense about'm, like the dogs or like kids."

He turns and looks very serious. "Let me tell you somethin', young man. If all our juries was made up of dogs and women and kids, justice would have its day in this country. They got a way of gettin' at the truth that don't no man have. Brang the accused into the courtroom in front of a jury of women, dogs, and kids, and wouldn't no lawyers have to be involved, none of that DDT testin' or whatever it's called. The judge'd ast, 'What

say you?' And they'd say 'Wudn't him' or 'He done
it.' The dogs'd just bark and growl if he was guilty,
wag their tails if he wudn't. That'd be it. Truth in
less than two minutes."

I begin to fidget and Winship pipes up: "Mr.
Pate, about the bowhunter's wife?"

"Oh yeah. Sorry. I got carried away. The little lady got it in her head that somethin' was up
and drove all the way from Houston to check it
out. Well, she parked around behind the cabins in
the mesquite trees and then went in the cabin he
was usin' and waited for him. Ain't no locks on the
doors."

"Usually nothing in them anybody'd steal
anyway," Winship says.

"Whatever," the old man continues, "long
about thirty minutes later he drove up with this
Ludy woman, that follered him in her car, and they
got out and started lockin' lips right there at the
truck, and he was pleadin' with her and all, but
she kept tellin' him that she had to get on to work.
Waitresses at the truck stop. But it looked like she
was maybe figgerin' she'd just go in a little late,
and they started torge the cabin."

"You gotta understand," Winship says, "that
Mr. Pate is not the sort of man who spies on other
people. He was just out checking his feeders."

"'At's a fact, I was. The one right behind that
cabin just happened to need checkin' that mornin'.
Anyway, in the mesquite thicket where I was at, I
never seen what happened when they walked thoo
that door, but I heard it. She must've been standin' right inside, against the wall, and when they
come in, she laid into that ol' boy with his own
damned bow. Ludy come out first, fell onto her all
fours, scrambled up, then hauled it to her car. He
busted thoo the door with his wife right behind
him swingin' that bow like a baseball bat. Sounded
like somebody whackin' a goose on the back with

a cane pole. Ludy must of seen some of it, but not much. She was flat on the way outta there. Laid a hell of a dust trail down the big road. Last I seen of him, he was scramblin' up on top of the truck and kickin' down at his wife, like you'd try to fend off a mad-dog. I cleared on out and got back to the house. About five minutes later the dogs started raisin' Cain and I heard his truck leave—in one big hurry."

"And her?"

He grins. "She come on out a little while later. When she drove by, I seen that she had bakin' soda all over what I could see of her—looked like she was decked out in white warpaint."

I look at Bob, then back to the old man. "Baking soda?"

"Yep," Bob says, "from the clothes bags. They pack their clothes in baking soda to kill the human smell—but that's a story for another day. We've got to get on back to the ranch before dark."

"I found out later that she had built a little fire up there in front of the cabin out of some thangs she thought needed burnin'—like a bornair and a whole bunch of camel-flogged clothes. I'm just glad she didn't figger the cabin had anythang to do with it."

Winship is cradling the fish skull in his hands. "Alas, poor Yorick," he begins, "I knew him, Ruffin, a man of infinite . . . ." Then: "I guess we need got to get on back over to the Rockpile."

"Yeah, I guess so."

The old man smiles again and shoots a stream of amber liquid way over into the yard. "Point is—" His voice trails off.

"Aw, we get your point, Mr. Pate, we get it," Winship is saying. He has a grin as big as the one on the bony lips of the fish.

I lean down and rub Ralph on the head. He doesn't even open an eye.

As we walk off through the low mesquite toward the road I say to Bob, "Hey, Winship. I dare you to go pet Judge." I can see the big black dog curled up at the foot of a gnarly mesquite tree. A large-link logging chain trails off in a shallow loop.

Winship stops and studies the dog. "How long has it been since you picked up a bow?"

I shrug. "Maybe twenty years, and it was a plain fiberglass re-curve. Forty, fifty-pound pull. Let me put it this way: A woman could have used it."

"You don't have a five-o'clock shadow, do you?"

"Only the one on the ground beside me."

He motions to me. "Come on then. We'll prove ourselves men or get killed."

Bob was an all-star football player for Rice back in the glory days of the early fifties when they won the Cotton Bowl, even signed a contract with the Philadelphia Eagles, so my shadow in the late sun is puny next to his as he walks straight as an arrow over to Judge, squats down before him, and strokes the dog's head. Judge rolls his eyes back and moans with pleasure as I lean over and rub his bony side.

"Ol' Pate's right—they know," Bob says. "Dogs know."

"I guess we've passed the test, huh?"

He smiles and pulls Judge's lip up to reveal a long white fang. "We still got to face the women. We're late for supper."

I nod and we rise and head on off down the dusty caliche road toward home.

The next day we're over at the Pate place again. Winship broke a handle on his posthole diggers and we've come over to borrow Mr. Pate's.

It's still morning, but conversations on his porch can happen anytime. The sky is a shocking blue, and the wind is playing up from the south today, soft and low like a cello. Mrs. Pate has brought out some cheese and crackers and iced tea, and we're having this sumptuous little feast for early lunch.

The old man holds up a cracker with a square of cheese on it and stares at it a long time, so I know his mind is on something. Yep: bowhunters.

But he doesn't say so right off. He just starts: "*Dummmmm . . . .*" His lips wrap the word up with a long, vibrant hum that he holds until I wonder when he'll come up for air. "They are, as a rule, the dumbest people you'll run into out here huntin'. Which is why they're good hunters—they think right down on the level of the creatures with hoofs. Which is why they got more patience than a rock. They don't think—they just set there and wait and watch. 'Bout as much sense as a cement block.

"Dumb as geese. And they are *dummmmmm-mm.*" He twists in his chair and looks at me. "One time I was comin' down Old Segovia Road, late of a winter night, ice and sleet and a dustin' of snow on everythang, and I come around a curve and seen five geese a-settin' right in the middle of road, asleep. They'd done landed on the road and thought it was a froze-over river. I coulda run right over'm. *Dummmmm . . . .*

"And most of'm couldn't track a freight train across them oat patches."

I just can't resist: "Why would you expect a goose to be able to track—"

"Ain't talkin' about no goose. Bowhunters is whut."

I thought he'd take it the way it was intended, as a joke, but sometimes he can be pretty literal in his thinking.

"One shot a Axis doe one time, real late, and

he lost it in the dark. Come by the house and tol' me he was gon' track it down the next mornin' Three days later he did. He come in proud as he could be and take'n me back up in the hills to where he had it field-dressed. When I examined it from the inside, I found two tight little holes on one side and two big old ragged holes on the other side where two bullets had went thoo the animal. You can tell arrer holes real well by the cross-slits the broad-heads make goin' in and out.

"Already stinkin' to high heaven. He'd tracked it down all right, by follerin' buzzards. And he went ahead and skinned it out. They gotta pertect their pride, you know."

Winship clears his throat. "Tell the Doc about the one who was going to live off the land."

Mr. Pate pivots toward Bob. "I don't remember no goose—"

"Naw, naw. That bowhunter."

Now the old man is turning it on us.

"That Patterson boy? Pumber out of Austin?"

"Yeah. He's the one."

"Turnt preacher, you know. After he got out of the pen."

"Yeah," Winship says, turning to me. "He found Jesus the second week in there, Ruffin, when a couple of guys cornered him and tried to get amorous."

I sip my coffee and say, "That would tend to make you religious."

"Got caught stealin' jurry and guns and stuff out of people's houses while he was plumbin'. Stole nearly a ten thousan' dollars worth from rich folks out at Lake Conroe. Way they caught him was the folks come home early and found him carryin' out a load of stuff in a wheelbarrel. It ain't exactly easy to explain away that sort of thang, so they sent him up. Preaches at some little church over in Louisianer."

"About his trying to live off the land . . . ."
Winship has to work to keep him on track.

"Well," Mr. Pate waxes, "Patterson's wife dropped him off out here one time to hunt for a week. Moved into the first cabin." He points toward the hunters' cabins. "I went up there the afternoon he moved in and talked thangs over with him, told him where the feeders was at and where I seen the biggest bucks lately.

"When I walked in the cabin, he was takin' his camel-flogs out of plastic bags and there was bakin' soda everwhere. Looked like he was gettin' ready to make biscuits or somethin'. You know, they pack their clothes in bakin' soda so they won't smell like humans, like we was talkin' about yesterday. Which never made any sense to me. Hell, you can't pack *yerself* in bakin' soda, and it's *you* that smells, not the clothes. You got to stay downwind is all, you know, and it don't matter what you smell like.

"Well, we talked on awhile about where he ought to hunt at, and I looked around and seen how little he'd done brought with him and ast him what he was gon' eat—I mean, he ain't brought grocery one with him, nothin', without you count that bakin' soda, not a can of beans or Wolf-brand chili, that I could see—and he just up and announced that he was gon' live off the land. For a week. Gon' shoot his food. Cook it right there in the hills. Like his forebears done.

"I wanted to say to him, 'Look, your forebears is dead, prolly *starved* to death, and it's all the ants can do out here to live off the land. Even buzzards got it hard.'

"You know how they always figgerin' on how many acres it takes to keep a cow alive out this way? Well, it takes forty acres per *buzzard* out here. At's how tough this land is to live off of.

"But I just ast him, 'You sure you want to try

this?' and he puffed his chest out and said, 'Yessir, I can do it.'

"Well, I done heard that tune before, and I always found out them ol' boys slipped off to the truck stop in the middle of the night—which this'n couldn't, without he was ready for a long walk, 'cause I sure as hell wudn't gon' drive him up there—and ate everthang but the tables and chairs. Waitress up there told me one time she seen a bowhunter fork in three platters of chicken-fried steak and French fries in less than half a hour—he'd been livin' off the land for a couple of days and I rekkin the livin' wudn't easy."

He motions toward the hills. "They's been times I coulda sold a can of sardines or a jar of peanut butter for ten dollars out there. Maybe fifty. So I says to this ol' boy, 'Me, I'd take a couple cans of Spam into the brush, just in case thangs don't go the way yer hopin'.

"'Nossir,' he said, 'I'll make do.'

"So I says to him, I says, 'Arright, you make all the do you want, but when you get to where you're just about too weak to move and might die any minute, you fire three shots in a row and I'll come runnin' with a samwich.'

"''Ain't gon' happen,' he said and he walked off toward the first clump of mesquites. Then he stopped and turned back to me.

"'If I get in trouble, you want me to fire three shots?'

"'Yep. That's the universal signal that you in trouble. Any fool knows that.'

"'Yessir. I know that. I'll remember that.' Then he walked off into the mesquite, disappeared."

The porch lapses into silence. I glance at Winship, then back to Mr. Pate. Far off an axis is yelping down in the river bottom.

Finally I ask, "So, uh, what about the rest of the story? Did the guy—"

"My point was how dumb they are, perfessor."

"I thought it was about not being able to live off the land."

"No. It was about how dumb they are. See, he walked off into the bushes and . . . ."

"Ruffin, Mr. Pate's point is that the guy was carrying a bow."

"Well, I *know* that. And he told him to fire three shots if . . . . Look, if he carried a *bow*, he could shoot all day and—"

"Now you got it," Winship says.

The old man just studies me.

On the way back along the dusty caliche road to the ranch we are quiet for a long way, down through the low-water crossing, where the water gurgles pleasantly beneath the concrete bridge, on up another stretch of lumpy road.

"He thought I was a fool, didn't he?" I ask finally.

"Naw, naw."

"I kept thinking about how stupid it was for him to tell the guy to shoot his bow three times for a distress signal, when what—when what he expected was—"

"Aw, he knows you're OK. He knows."

I have the heavy steel post-hole diggers slung over my shoulder like a rifle, and my shadow rippling along beside me reminds me of something I simply cannot name.

A Thanksgiving Story

We were talking turkeys. Mr. Pate has herds of them. I once slipped up to the edge of a bluff overlooking a couple of his oat patches and counted over sixty in one drove. It is serious turkey country.

"The one thang ever bowhunter has just got to do . . . ," the old man is saying over a beer. It's late and we've been sitting on his porch listening to a couple of gobblers jawing at each other off in a patch of low-growing mesquite. "He's got to kill a turkey." He struggles to relight his pipe in a stiff breeze up from the river. Puffs and snorts and coughs. "Got to get a bird. Almost like it's wrote in the Bible that he's got to."

He leans back and takes a deep draw on his pipe. On the darkening porch the bowl flares and glows and bathes his face in baptismal light. "There was this guy named Jenkins used to bowhunt out here. Wadn't worth a damn with a bow or anythang else I ever seen him use—he sure as hell couldn't use a axe. I seen him one time try to split—"

"Mr. Pate," Winship interrupts.

"Oh yeah. Lost track. Well, he'd been tryin' all October and November to nail a turkey for Thanksgivin'. Done tol' the wife and kids he was gon' brang one in for the table, not to go out and buy no Butterball or nothin'—the bird was *his* department.

"He musta got two dozen shots and never so much as floated a feather. I seen him shoot into a flock of at least twenty right under one of the feeders out there and them clumped up thick enough you couldn't a-throwed a rock in there without killin' at least two. It was just one big bunch of turkey. He didn't hit nothin' but ground.

"Well, it was gettin' closer and closer to Thanksgivin' and Jenkins didn't have no turkey for the table. Walks up to me in the yard one day and says, 'What am I gon' do, Mr. Pate? I got to get a bird.' So I says back, 'Me, I'd kill one with a rifle and then run a arrer thoo the bullet hole. Won't nobody know but you and me, and I won't tell.'

"That got the wheels to turnin' in his head, a-course, so he take'n my old Sprangfield with some military ball ammo that wouldn't expand and blow the bird to smithereens and hunted them fields and bluffs for the three days leadin' up to Thanksgivin', and wouldn't you know them turkeys would choose that exact time to go on vacation. Smart birds, you know. He never seen turkey one!

"So he comes onto the porch here the day before Thanksgivin' all hangdog, hands me the rifle, says he rekkins he's whupped, gon' go on home to the fambly without a bird."

I look at Winship, then back at the old man. "Did he?"

"Not a chanch," Mr. Pate says. "I tell him to come on in and set down and I says to him, 'Here's what you do—'"

Jenkins left the house that day in a little better mood, drove to the big Super S in Junction, and came back with something in a paper bag and stopped just a second to talk to Mr. Pate before going on up to one of the hunters' cabins.

"What was in the bag?" I ask.

"Big Butterball," Winship says.

Mr. Pate relights his pipe, draws deeply, then

exhales a cloud of blue smoke. "Yeah, prolly weighed fifteen pounds, the biggest one in the bin."

I laugh. "OK. I think I know where this is going. He tries to pass this turkey off as one he's killed, right?"

"Ayup," Mr. Pate grunts. "That he did."

Wiship clears his throat. "See, bowhunters have an enormous amount of pride, and this Jenkins guy was no exception. He said he would have a turkey for Thanksgiving, and he did. The biggest one he could find. He took the turkey up to the cabin and put it in the shower and ran hot water on it until he figured it was thawed . . . ."

Mr. Pates laughs. "At's a big tank there, and even *it* couldn't keep up. I 'spect he run nearly a thousand gallons of water and burnt a lot of cubit feet of propane to soften thatere bird. He damn near cooked it right there in the shower, and I guarantee you *he* ain't never been that clean since he was a baby."

Winship picks up: "When he judged he'd thawed the turkey out enough to shoot an arrow through it, he took it out and set it on a sawhorse and stood back a couple of dozen feet and let fly with a broadhead."

Mr. Pate claps his hands together. "*Chunk*! Sounded like he done shot a piece of granite. I seen him do it. Heard him do it."

"It didn't go through?"

"Why, hell no, it never went thoo. A arrer can't go thoo a block of solid ice. He yanked it out and looked at them curled blades and take'n the bird back into the shower stall for another hour or so, then come back out and set it on the sawhorse and shot it again, and this time the arrer went halfway thoo the breast and glanced off that core of ice and went on over in the mesquites."

"So he fooled his family into thinking he'd killed the turkey."

"Well, that's what he told'm when he got the bird home. Told'm he just cleaned it here at the ranch. And a-course everbody just went hog-wild as jackasses over what a big turkey Daddy done kilt. They's on the phone half the night callin' members of the fambly over in Mississippi."

"Well," I say, "I know this is leading some-where, but—"

"Where it's leading to," Winship says, "is the next day when they've got that great big turkey laid out on the table for carving."

"Aw, I got it. He forgot to removed the ther-mometer from the breast."

Winship snorts. "Naw, naw: Mr. Pate told him to pry that out first thing."

"Then where's the—"

"Mr. Pate'll tell you. This is his porch and his privilege."

The old man grunts and shifts in his lawn chair, scraping it across the stone floor. "At's a fact." He smiles big. "The little lady carved the tur-key—well, actually she ain't little at all, really a *big* woman, one I wouldn't want to run up against at a beer joint, great big ol' arms . . ."

"Mr. Pate." Winship tries to steer him back on course.

"Yeah, yeah. Hadn't been for her tellin' my wife, wouldn't nobody know. Well, when she take'n a slice acrost that big old fat Butterball breast, the knife struck somethin'. It'uz a blade of one of them broadheads. She helt it up and looked real close at it. 'Holy cow,' Jenkins says, 'I ain't never had one break off like that in a turkey before,' to which she replies, just loud enough for him to hear but not the chilren, 'Gerald, it wouldn't have if you'd let it get full thawed before you shot it.'"

I roar at that, figuring it's the end of the story, but Winship motions with his hands that there's more.

"Later on," Mr. Pate continues, "they're a-settin' at the table after the chilren are outside playin' and he's sorta sheepish about the whole thang, head down, peepin' at her ever now and then, like a little boy been caught stealin' or lookin' up some girl's dress or jerkin' off, but she's doin' what women always do, nursin' his ego along, tellin' him it's all right.

"'Naw, it ain't,' Jenkins tells her, 'I lied to you about that bird.' She reaches out and pats him on the arm, says to'm, 'Now, Gerald, I had that figgered out purty early on.' And he asts her how could that be, and she says, 'Well, you done a real good job cleanin' him.'

"He nods and thanks her, and she says, 'But not many men'd be thoughtful enough to wrap the turkey's neck up in a little package with the gizzard and liver and shove it up his ass.'"

I lose the last word as my beer spews out across the floor. Mr. Pate swings off on another tangent about how any man would be a fool to try to trick a woman with a Butterball turkey. "They know Butterballs better'n them Butterball people knows Butterballs . . . ." His voice trails off as Winship tries to resuscitate me.

The Great Camel Experiment

"Yeah, I've heard about them. My friend Eddie Weems filled me in in a bar in Waco a few years ago, only he embellished the story so much that I didn't know what was true and what was not."

I am responding to Mr. Pate's question about whether I've heard about the camel experiment our Army conducted in Texas back in the 1850s. We're on his front porch, as usual, and the sun is hammering down in West Texas fashion, driving most sensible creatures to shade. And to beer, if they are lucky enough to have some on hand, as the old man always does. Bob Winship is with me, and we are all sipping suds while Mrs. Pate finishes up a pie she's about to slide into the oven and share with us when it's done. Blackberry.

"They was headquartered, them camels was, just a few miles from here, over at Camp Verde, in the bottom part of Kerr County, just a few miles south of Kerrville, near Bandera Pass. They run a few expeditions with'm out of there, and one time they take'n a pack of'm all the way to California."

"Eddie said they brought them in at Indianola, somewhere near Corpus Christi."

"Naw, Indianoler was, or *is*, on Matagorder Bay near Port Lavahker, which is right at halfway between Galveston and Corpus. Ain't much of it left now, since the Yankees blowed the bejeezus out of it durin' the War of Northern Aggression, and then it got hit by a harric'n and then got hit by a bad fahr that purty much burnt up what the storm didn't get. It wudn't really a hell of a good place to be from."

"Eddie said they didn't last very long, that the Army just gave up on them."

"Well, it wudn't many left, after the harric'n and fahr. I mean, would you stay in a bad-luck place like that?"

"I was talkin' about the camels."

"The camels?"

"Yessir. The camels. Why did the Army give up on the camels?"

"Well, for one thang, they ugly as hell, camels are, and they are stubborn, and they don't ever forget anythang you do to'm that they figger you shouldn't, and they stink real bad. And word is that if you mess with one, he will wait forever for the chanch to kick your brains out or spit on you." He cocks an eye toward the screen door, beyond which Mrs. Pate is humming "Amazing Grace" and puttering about the kitchen. "Or piss all over you."

"*Piss* all over you?"

"Kinda like Faulkner's mule," Winship puts in. "He'll wait a lifetime to get a chance to kick you if he doesn't like you. But mules don't spit, and I've never heard of one pissing on anybody either."

"What Faulkner?" the old man asks.

"William," Bob says, but it's totally wasted on Mr. Pate, who doesn't know William Faulkner from Toady Falkner, who runs an auto-repair shop in Junction and has never read a book, much less written one.

"Accordin' to all I been able to find out about it, they brought in 33 of them in 1855, and then another 41 a little later. Why them odd numbers, I don't know. I'd of rounded it off to 30 and 40 myself, but I wudn't around to give'm advice. They unloaded them at Indianoler and marched them up to Camp Verde—which, as I was sayin', is where the Camel Corps was assembled. From there they take'n off on the different expeditions the Army sent'm on. The main driver was a guy by the name of Hi Jolly."

"Hadji Ali was his Arabic name," Winship puts in, "but you can imagine how long that pronunciation lasted around those soldiers."

He continues: "In 1855 Congress appropriated $30,000 to fund an experiment with camels in the Great American Desert, since Army horses and mules were having a really hard time with the terrain. Jefferson Davis was Secretary of War at the time, and the Army wanted animals capable of carrying a heavy burden and that didn't need water every day. So, with Davis pushing the plan, Congress came up with the money, and the government sent a ship to the Middle East in search of camels, which they found in Egypt. They went with the two-humped ones, which could carry a heavier load than the one-humped ones."

"And they brought'm in at Indianoler, and then take'n'm overland to Camp Verde.

"It seems to me like a reasonable project to me," I say. "What went wrong?"

"What went wrong," the old man says, taking a heavy slug of beer, "is that nobody involved in the experiment had bothered to figger out just how different camels is than the horses and mules they was sposed to replace. They are one of the ugliest critters on earth for one thang, and they are mean-spirited. And they got a real peculiar odor.

"Them camels didn't want to be over here anymore than most of the people here wanted'm here, so they just bowed up and decided to be uncooperative. They could haul a thousand pounds of stuff on they backs and tote it over fifty miles a day, and they could go three days without water, but they just had a bad attitude, which any of us might have if we'd a-been drug all the way over here to a strange land amongst strange people and animals. They scared the total hell out of ever mule and horse that seen'm or that just happened to be downwind of'm, and not even dogs would come near'm. Word is that even the Indians was scared of'm and wouldn't kill and eat one. When a Indian won't eat a piece of meat, there's got to be somethin' bad wrong with it.

"When the Army camel colyums come near a strang of prospecters or whatever, the camels would figger there was corn or some kinda grain in the caravan and haul it torge the mules pullin' the wagons and scare'm to death, and the mules'd bolt and turn over wagons and scatter stuff everwhere. Them mules had never saw anythang like them ugly-ass camels before, so the onliest thang they knowed to do was hit the road, Jack, which they done.

"The prospecters take'n to shootin' the camels, which didn't create a whole lot of what you might call good will between the civilian colyums and the military, so it was just a matter of time before somebody had to yield. Another prollem was that camel toes is real bad about pickin' up rocks. Hi Jolly started wroppin' they feet with burlap, but they'd wear that out real quick—imagine camel toes grindin' against rocks with nuthin' but burlap in between . . . ."

It's hard to keep a straight face imagining that, but I do.

"Finally the Army had some shoes built for'm, but you can imagine what a devil of a time you'd have puttin' shoes on camels. Just try it on a *mule* and see what kind of behavior you get. You just about got to tie a mule's legs and lay him over to do it.

"Well, eventually the Army decided it just wudn't worth goin' on with the experiment, so they called the whole thang off. It didn't matter that the camels could haul half a ton of goods and go three days without water if they scared the total hell out of everythang they come across, so the Army just shut the Camel Corps down and turnt the animals aloose in Arizona and California and let'm go it on they on. I heard tell that to this day they's people with a eye out for camels in the Great American Desert. Matter of fact, they's a guy name Keiser out in Arizona that has devoted the rest of his life to findin' the offsprang of them original camels out there. He says he seen the tracks of one once but ain't caught sight of a real one yet."

"What would he do if he found one?"

"Well, Perfesser, you'll have to ask him. Me, I'd just take me one good look and let it go at that."

So I let it go at that and settle back in my chair and sip on my beer, wondering just what I'm going to learn on this porch next time.

The Tent Revival Goiter

According to Mrs. Pate, who has lately returned to something resembling a regular pattern in church attendance, at a revival meeting back in late August the roving evangelist, a converted convict down from the High Plains, got handed a problem he couldn't deal with, hard as he tried.

"A *what?*"

"A goider."

Hell, I know what a goiter is. I'm just wondering how one got into this conversation. But, then, I know not to be surprised by anything that pops up on this porch.

"A woman I know showed up from out around Telegraph, south a'here, with a goider the size of a teenage armadiller, lots bigger'n a goiderette, and ast could he heal her of it. They's some faith healin' still goes on, you know, even out here, where it's mostly retarred people from Houston or Santone that don't even believe in Heaven and Hell, much less faith healin'. I'm not sure that they even believe in God, most of'm. Just money and fine cars and houses and such."

She runs her tongue across her barren gums. "And a full set a'teef."

"Ma'am?" I don't know how many teeth she has salvaged from whatever fate befell their mouth mates, but since the ones she has are somewhere way back in there beyond seeing, except in little yellow flashes when she laughs or talks while she's chewing, she has trouble with the *th* sound, so it's not that I don't understand the word. It's that I don't get the connection between a full set of *teef* and a *bleef* in God.

"Most of'm has got full sets," she says, "and lots of them teef was made in a shop somewhere, not put there by God. Inplants and stuff like that. Plates. Bridges. Lotsa gold and silver in they moufs."

"Yes'm." I shift and pick up my glass of tea and take a swig. "But I'd really like to hear the goiter story."

Well, it seems that this evangelist named Hoggard wheeled down out of Lubbock and arrived one Monday morning and by mid-afternoon had a sawdust oval laid and a tent erected, with over a hundred folding chairs lined up in front of a raised platform with a cross-shaped podium, in front of which was a big clearing. Anyone who's ever attended a genuine tent revival meeting knows what the clearing is for.

She nods toward Mr. Pate, who's in earnest conversation at the other end of the porch with Winship, who's over with me, as usual. "Delbert seen it and told me about it when he got home, and I called Margie Praeter down at the church—she's the secretary and has got a nose as long as yer arm and don't mind puttin' it in other people's binness and knows everthang that happens in the valley—and ast did they know anythang about it, and she said no, but she would in a little bit. And shernuff, in less than a'hour Margie called back and said it was a Reverend Parsley Hoggard from some little town near Amariller and he come down on his own, not invited by no church whatsoever and dropped by and got a permit from somebody at the city—prolly bribed somebody, like they do down in Mexico—

and there he was. Hired him some trash in town to set up the tent and all them chairs. Margie said he didn't have no church afflict . . . affa . . . effe . . . ."

It sounds like she's about to sneeze, so I help her out: "Affiliation."

"At's it. He was non-dominational."

"Denomi—" But I just shut up, knowing it won't penetrate, just bounce like a forty-yard BB off a cow.

"Now, Perfesser, I've heard you tell about witnessin' faith healin' and such when you was growin' up, and like that I said, it still goes on, even out here, and there he was with that big ol' tent set up and signs all over town declarin' that beginnin' the next night—that'd been Tuesday—he was goin' to commence savin' and healin' people of their affi . . . affel . . . afflictions."

I marvel at how she got through the word without more than a couple of little stumbles.

"Big red signs with black letters tellin' about hell and sickness and all. And how if you was possessed by demons, he could cast'm ass-under."

I laugh and look at Winship, who's picked up on part of the conversation. "*Asunder*," he mouths. I nod. I used to think the preacher was saying *ass-under* too.

"And how if you was a sick and shut-in, he could make you well. And save you from hell if you turnt yer heart over to God or Jesus and yer money over to him. And all that stuff. Signs everwhur."

I'm finishing off my second glass of tea and wondering where exactly the goiter fits in. Winship and Mr. Pate have left the front porch and gone out to inspect one of their cages designed to catch cowbirds. Winship never did express any interest in goiters, even with his medical training.

"Had'm in ever store front and tacked to sticks drove into the ground, with arrers and everthang, like anybody in Junction could miss a tent the size of a big barn, especially when they kick that music up, the way they always do. It's the music that makes people do crazy thangs at tent revivals. What it does to they eardrums and all and they brains, ain't no tellin'. It ain't the spirit they feelin'—it's the music that's vibratin' they insides right down to they souls."

"Yes'm, been there," I say. "That music'll loosen up pocketbooks too."

"Shoooo, I rekkin. I seen farmers tight as a turnip go a-reachin' for they cash when they jack that music up and the preacher gets red-faced and loud as a mule beller."

"Mrs. Pate . . . ."

She sighs and sits forward in her chair. "I know, I know. Yonta hear about the goider."

"Yes'm."

Well, it seems that by Thursday word about the revival had gotten out all over Kimble County, and people were beginning to drive in to witness some of the miracles unfolding under the big tent, especially the laying on of hands and healing, which they found infinitely more interesting than the same old platitudes and parables they had paraded before them every week in church. It was one thing to hear about ancient miracles, quite another to see one occur *amongst* them in the *fuh-lesh-uh*, which is the way the preachers of my youth pronounced the word.

The crowd Tuesday, the first night of the revival, was not much of a crowd at all, more like a gathering of gawkers, as Mrs. Pate put it. The first two rows of folding chairs were filled, with a smattering of souls in the middle and toward the back, but by Thursday night, the big top was jammed with people, from whining babies to ancient crones, wheeled in to witness a miracle and maybe even be part of one.

Typically, most of the evening was devoted

to fervent preaching by Reverend Hoggard, whose reputation flowed down from Lubbock like a roil of molasses right off the stove, sweet and thick and warm, for he was a man who focused on love and forgiveness rather than sin and retribution, and he painted Heaven in cool blue with the same conviction that most revival evangelists broadstroked Hell in red. And so it was that even children loved to hear him go on about what Paradise was like for those who followed the brighter path upward instead of the dark path down to the *Pitta Fahr*, as he pronounced it.

He didn't even leave the impression that all God's children would stand around in Heaven in choir robes singing hymns all day. He just told people that in Heaven all their wishes could be fulfilled. That's the kind of slant on Heaven even *I* could have bought into as a boy. Girls, fried chicken, ice cream, football—those are just some of the things I'd have wished for.

Ah, but it was the miracles they were there for, young and old and in-between, the laying on of hands that turned bent and broken bodies into sprightly, nimble creatures that danced across the stage after Brother Hoggard's healing touch. They wanted *miracles*.

And miracles they got. Every night, after the sermon and much music, after the swelling of spiritual and material coffers, the Greatest Show on Earth began. When beseeched by the Reverend, those with afflictions rose from the audience and limped and stumbled and tapped their way into the line that led to the stage where they would clump up wooden steps, some barely able to drag themselves along, and stand before the man down from the High Plains who would, with help from Someone from a Higher Plain, make them whole again.

"Healed cripples and blind people and the

deef," Mrs. Pate says. "Even them with the cancer or sugar di-beetees or the yeller jundis. It was one woman come in with the yeller jundis so bad she was the color of a arnge. She come back the next night pink as a baby's butt."

Before the evening was over, the sawdust semicircle before the stage would be filled with crutches and dark glasses, canes and hearing aids, enough for a good garage sale, as Mrs. Pate puts it.

She pivots in her chair and squints over at me. "But all them people that was healed was strangers to the local folk. Ain't nobody I talked to ever seen *any* of'm before."

"Bussed'm in?"

"Whut I figger. Nobody knowed nary a one of them. Had to of come from somewhere outta town."

"But what about the goiter?" I ask her. I mean, the goiter is what kicked this whole thing into motion. You can't throw that kind of thing into a conversation without fleshing it out.

"Well . . . ." She settles back in her chair and drapes her ample arms across her even ampler chest. "Miz Tutwiler, from down around Telegraph, like that I said earlier, made the trip all the way up to Junction because her husband said there was a good chanch she could get her goider shucked off by the preacher and they wouldn't have to spend a fortune havin' it cut off at the hospital. I mean, it ain't like they are a serious affliction or anythang, but they scare chirren sometimes, and older kids'll laugh and point at'm in public. So why not get it took off by the preacher? You know, he'd lay a hand on her forehead and say *HEAL!* and then peel that sucker off like a big leech and thowe it right out there with the crutches and stuff."

"And?"

"Well, she arose and lined up with the others, and he healed ever sangle one that crossed the stage in front of her, includin' a colored man with a limp so bad his wife had to help him up on the stage, only Reverend Hoggard looked real puzzled when she showed up before him." She grins big. "It was like he hadn't figgered on her bein' in the line." She cackles, then gets serious.

"Joyceanne—at's her first name, Jones is her last, I bleeve—just pointed to the goider and ast him to heal her of it, and, Perfesser, he looked the way Raynette might look at a math prollem, like she ain't got the foggiest notion how to go about solvin' it, which she wouldn't. He re-*coiled* from it is whut he done. He acted like it had teef or somethin' and was gon' bite him. Turnt pale, like she had a demon on her neck. He backed up and motioned for the music to start up again, and then he he turnt to the congregation and started prayin', with Joyceanne standin' there under them lights and nobody knowin' what to do. He kep' on prayin' and the music kep' goin' until the line behind her just kinda dissolved, and she turnt around and stomped off the stage and went right to the truck, with Mr. Tutwiler taggin' along behind like a dog that ain't real sure whut's in store for him when he gets home. And she's big enough to where she could cause him some real damage if she was amind to. Humiliatin' is whut it was. She'll get over it. The humiliatin', I mean, not the goider. Them thangs hang on forever, whut I've heard."

"So . . . what happened?"

"Well, they wasn't but a handful of people there Friday night, and by midday Saredy they wasn't nothin' on the lot but that big patch of sawdust wif some crutches and canes and stuff in pile in front of where the stage was at."

"So the Reverend Hoggard hauled it back to Lubbock, did he?"

"Yep. Tucked his tail and run is the way that

Margie put it. She got a way wif words, she does. She says he's prolly prayin' real hard on how to handle goiders or is on the Internet studyin' up on how to heal somebody of one."

"I 'spect so," I say. "I 'spect so."

Raynette's Got a Prollem

Winship and I are perched on Mr. Pate's front porch, the three of us enjoying some beer and cigars before Mrs. Pate joins us, at which time the cigars have to be doused and the beer shared with yet another person. She never has more than two, but she will have those, come hail or high water, unless serious man talk or bad language keeps her inside.

The subject has been weather, a fairly frequent topic, but Winship has just asked Mr. Pate to tell me about his great-grandson's new girlfriend. The two of them were out the week before, since Junior got an itch to shoot an Axis deer and the old man made the mistake of telling him that he'd seen one with three-foot beams in one of the oat patches for four nights hand-running, as Mrs. Pate is apt to phrase it. She's just come out onto the porch and plopped down in her lawn chair. It's one of those old metal types with the arms that curl down and loop around in a *U* shape to form the base. It settles a good four inches when she sits down. Needs a good set of shock absorbers.

The wise old head pivots like an owl's. "Hmm-mmm? Oh, you talkin' about Raynette. Oh, yeah. That Raynette. She's somethin'. She speaks with a fork-ed tongue."

I look at Winship, then back to the old man.

"Do you mean she lies or what?" Mrs. Pate is quietly snickering. I can tell by the way her belly jiggles.

"I mean that she speaks with a *fork-ed* tongue is whut I mean."

I turn back to Winship. "Any enlightenment here?"

"Like he says, Raynette speaketh with a fork-ed tongue. I saw it myself."

"OK, somebody's got to clue me in here. I know what it means to speak with a fork-ed tongue. I am one-eighth Cherokee, and I have occasionally spoken with a fork-ed tongue. But what do you mean when you say you *saw* it? Heard it I can understand. Saw it I cannot."

"The girl's tongue has been sliced so that she has a tongue that looks like a snake's," Winship says. "Only it's split from the tip right on back to where it attaches, I guess."

"Do you mean her tongue has actually been cut in half, lengthwise?"

"At's a fact," Mrs. Pate confirms.

"She have an accident?"

"Nope. Not without you count it a accident for her to be born dumb as she is. She went to a tattoo poller and got her tongue cut right down the middle."

I look from one to the other and reach for another beer. "Well, what the hell for?"

"There's your buck-fifty question," the old man says. "She said they didn't even use nothin' to deaden it with either. Done it in stages. Give her a coupla shots of whiskey and heated one of them Exacto knifes with a cigarette lighter and wiped it off with alkyhawl and sliced her tongue about half a inch each trip so she wouldn't bleed too much. Dobbed off the blood a few times and turned her aloose. She'd heal up, and they'd cut again. Finally they had the whole thang cut right down the middle. "

"Uh, Bob," I appeal to Winship, "tell me this is not so."

"Oh, it's so," he says. "It's the new rage. Gotta top the body piercing and tattoos, you know. They call it body modification, or mutilation. Means the same thing."

"You're serious about this? I thought butt rings were pretty much the lunatic fringe of things, but this . . . ."

"Whut in the world is a *butt* rang?" the old man asks.

"Well, I've never seen one, but I hear that they are rings made out of brass or something, maybe two inches or so in diameter, and these kids get their buttocks pierced and the rings inserted."

"Looks like it'd hurt to set down," Mrs. Pate says.

"It probably does. It's a California thing."

"Might know," the old man says.

But I want to know more about Raynette's tongue, so I ask.

Mr. Pate laughs, a kind of a rumble from way deep in his chest. "Raynette, she does this thang to Junior from across the room with her tongue that if a man did that to a woman out somewhere he'd get his jaws slapped clean off, but Junior gets a kick out it, like it's somethin' real private between'm and prolly is, and she looks just lak a snake testin' the air when she does it."

Mrs. Pate kicks in: "If the Good Lord had of meant for us to have split tongues, he'd a took away our shoulders and arms and feet and give us scales and cold blood. Lots of groundwork for mankind was laid in the Garden, but split tongues wudn't one of'm.

"I tol' Junior that someday he gon' have to get that thang sewed up and won't no tattoo poller man be able to do that. Gon' take a man in a white coat with a whole bunch of diplomers on his wall.

Somebody in a white coat is gon' get her anyhow. Point is, it's gon' cost'm some real money."

She turns in her lawn chair and levels her eyes at me. "I mean, Perfesser, when Raynette goes and interviews for a job, who you rekkin can take her serious with her tongue flappin' all over the place?"

"Winship, can a person even talk with a split tongue?"

"A crow can," Mr. Pate says. "That's how you can get one to talk."

Winship looks sagely. "I have heard Raynette speak, and I gotta tell you, Ruffin, it is not what I would call birdsong. She's having to learn how to talk all over. Think how important the tongue is to speaking. It's at least half of articulation."

"Raynette, she got herself a long row to hoe," Mrs. Pate says, then gets up and goes inside.

"If you guys are yanking my leg . . . ."

"It's the God's honest truth, Perfesser," the old man assures me. "Sure's I'm settin' here drankin' this beer on my porch, my great-grandson is goin' with a girl with a fork-ed tongue. I just wish you could see it in person."

Mrs. Pate is suddenly back on the porch, this time with a frosted mug to pour her beer into. "We seen a pitcher of somebody that had it done on the internet. He had one half of his tongue wropped round the other, like they was tusslin', said he could move both sides of his tongue, in differnt directions." She settles back into her lawn chair, which squawks for good reason, and grins. "Both sides. We in the end times is whut."

"He had it done on the internet?" I mean it as a joke.

"Naw, naw, Perfesser," Mr. Pate says, "we *seen* him on the internet is whut she's tryin' to say. Had this boy, a teenager, showin' off his split tongue like he was proud of it, and I guess he was.

The guy that was interviewin' him—it was all he to do to keep from havin' a laughin' fit. He ast the boy could he tie it in a knot without usin' his fangers, and he said he might could but hadn't tried that yet."

And then the whole thing just seems to settle into perspective. The world is dropping into night again, as it does so wonderfully every evening out here, and the four of us quietly sip our beer and watch the advancing purple shadows that slide off the cliffs and fill the valley.

There are times that I feel totally out of tune with the outer world. This is one of them.

A few months later. Same setting.

It's been a splendid day out here in the valley, and we're kicked back sipping suds—Winship, Mr. Pate, and I—while Mrs. Pate takes a look in the oven at whatever kind of dish she's whipped up for supper. The woman can make a casserole out of anything that ever ran or flew or swam or just lay there waiting to be picked up and put to culinary use.

When she gets back to the porch and settles into her lawn chair and the groaning of the metal has stopped, I ask what she is cooking and she says a casserole, fleshed out with a jackrabbit that her great-grandson shot out by the barn. "It don't no kind of meat goes to waste around here," she says with satisfaction and pops her gums together to punctuate.

"Are you talking about Raynette's boyfriend?" Winship asks her.

"Fersher. Junior. Only they married now. Got hitched a few weeks ago." After a pause she adds, "And Raynette's got a prollem."

I sip my beer and hold the bottle up and

steady it like I'm setting it on the top of the bluff across the river.

"What kind?" I ask. "She still having trouble with her tongue?" Raynette's tongue-split was supposed to add a dimension of mystique to her, but she has had a lot of trouble with it. As far as I am concerned, Raynette needs other dimensions worse.

"Naw, they got it whipstitched back together somewhere over in San Antonio, since she was havin' trouble at her new job at a cowpracter's office."

The old man pops up in his chair. "*Kiro*-practer. *Kiro*. Like the syrup or the town in Egypt. He don't have shit to do with no cows. Can't you just see this guy workin' his way thoo yer herd, poppin' they backs?"

"You stop cussin'. You know how I hate that. And it is *Kay*-ro syrup, not *Kiro*. So you don't know everthang. But *Kiro*-practer, then, if it'll make you feel any better. Whatever one is called, she gotta talk on the phone a lot, and people was havin' trouble understandin' what she was sayin'. She couldn't talk worf beans before she got it split. Sounded like some kinda sick bird after. Well, sicker than before." She sighs. "At any rate, they got it sewed up."

"So what's her problem this time?" I ask.

"Well," the old woman says, "she got thowed off a horse up in the rocks and fell on her butt real hard and she's got to have a tubal libation."

I just stare at her a few seconds, then at Winship, who has the courtesy not to guffaw.

Then Mr. Pate gets on it. "*Litigation*," he says. "She can't pronounce *crap* right."

She levels her eyes at him. "*Cuh-rap*," she says. "Was that right, you old *fahrrrt*?"

"By George, she's got it," Winship says, his whole face beaming. Then, since he's been to medical school, he settles the issue: "*Ligation.* The word you are searching for is *ligation.* She had her tubes tied."

The old man ignores Winship and stares at his wife. "*Now* who's cussin'?"

"The word *fart* is not cussin'. It is a scientific term. It's in the dictionary."

"So is *shit*," he says, "but ever time *I* say that word, I get yelled at."

"Shit is not scientific, even if it *is* in the dictionary."

"And just what makes *fart* scientific and *shit* not?"

"I heard tell is all."

"You don't know *shit* about—"

"I think Ruffin would like to hear about Raynette's new problem," Winship sugggests.

The old woman ceases glaring at Mr. Pate, then nods. "That's what they done all right. Tied'm off. Now her eggs can't get down there to where she can get pregnant."

"I don't see why falling off a horse would necessitate a tubal ligation," I say.

"Ownknow how come she was on a horse anyhow," Mr. Pate says. "She so addled she can barely ride a school bus."

"Well, I don't know how it done it," Mrs. Pate says with an air of finality, "but it did. The doctors said she shouldn't have no babies."

The old man has had some four beers by now, and he's obviously agitated. He clears his throat and says, "First thang I want to know is how they tie them tubes off. They just cinch'm up with catgut or whut? They cut'm first?"

Winship snorts. "Catgut?" Then: "Well, they can fuse the fallopian tubes with cauterization or suture them or use clips of some sort. Sometimes they will also remove a section of the tubes to be certain that a splice doesn't develop naturally."

But he realizes that he's already about half a mile over the old man's head, so he concludes: "Yes, they cinch'm up . . . with catgut."

"Another thang I want to know is whut happens to them eggs that stacks up in there." He looks at Winship for an answer again. Bob just studies his beer.

"Looks like to me that once you drop down so many and they're backed up like peas in a pod, somethin' in there would have to give. Explode maybe. You know what I mean? Let's say a dozen eggs . . . ."

He looks over at Winship again. "How big is them thangs anyhow?"

"What?" Bob asks him. "How big is *what*?"

"Them eggs. They the size of hen eggs or whut?"

"They are microscopic, they are so small." Then he sees the old woman, who's been amazingly quiet with all this female plumbing discussion going on, wrinkle her forehead. "You cannot see them with the naked eye. Like sperm." Then: "They are tiny, about the size of mouse eggs."

Mrs. Pate adjusts her enormous bottom in the chair. "A mouse don't lay no eggs. I might not know much, but I know *that*. I'd of seen'm."

"I didn't say that they *lay* them. They don't *lay* eggs, anymore than a woman does, but they *produce* them."

"Well," she says and rises to address the casserole, "Raynette's eggs, whether they the size of a mouse egg or the size of a rooster egg, ain't gonna drop down far enough now to where any little wigglers can get to'm. Like I done said lots of times before, Raynette has got herself a long row to hoe, like from here to San Antonio."

After that the conversation drops off to nothing and Winship and I say our goodbyes and head back to the Rockpile, afoot as usual.

"Didn't want any jackrabbit stew, Bob?"

"Nope," he says. "You couldn't tenderize a jackrabbit with a grenade. Only a whole herd of eighteen-wheelers and that hot Texas sun on asphalt can do it right."

"I don't know about you, but I feel a whole lot better about the future of the country knowing that Raynette has had her tubes tied."

"Me too," he says. A few seconds later: "Ruffin, you ever get the idea that you're coming back from the Twilight Zone when we leave that place?"

"Just about every time, Bob, just about every time."

The Nighturnal Remnant

"You want to see him?" the old man asks.

"Sure," I say. Winship, who's with me, nods.

So we leave the porch and follow him out into the scrub mesquite until we're standing before a little mesh-wire trap-cage that Mr. Pate bought at the hardware store. It's the kind that you put bait in the rear of and cock open a metal flap for entry. Maybe three feet long, a foot tall and wide. When the animal goes in for the bait, he steps on a trip plate and the flap clangs down behind him. It's good for possums or coons or cats or small dogs, anything that can fit through the opening. The way you catch what you're after is by putting the right kind of bait in there. Sometimes that's the real tricky part, Mr. Pate has explained, since something like a possum or an armadillo will eat almost anything under the sun or stars or cloudy sky.

The bait this time was a clutch of alfalfa, which might sound rather odd, since most animals that eat alfalfa couldn't get much more than a leg into the trap and wouldn't try even that. I mean, how could they scoop it up? The hoof isn't particularly good for grasping, never was meant to be. He has caught what he was after: a possum. But not just any possum. This is the strangest creature you might ever encounter amongst all of God's chirren.

A little background is necessary here. One evening back last fall Mr. Pate was in one of his deer blinds scoping out a particular feeder, which had gone off at five o'clock, as it was set to do. A little click and whir and corn is slung in a broad band around the base of the feeder, and any deer in the neighborhood recognizes that as the sound of a dinner bell and will ease up and nibble away. While he is so engaged, whoever's in the stand has a nice, easy shot. I remarked one time that it didn't sound very sporting, but Mr. Pate pointed out that running deer with dogs in Mississippi and shooting them with buckshot when they broke out of cover didn't sound all that sporting either, so I shut up for a minute. Then I pointed out what John Wesley Hardin had to say about hunting—that there was no sport in any kind of hunting when the hunted can't shoot back—to which the old man replied that he had tried for years to arm the deer, but they never took him up on the idea. Said he even tried to keep and arm bears—I'm pretty sure that was a joke.

At any rate, half an hour or so after the feeder went off, some kind of animal came waddling out of the brush and started having supper, so the old man laid his rifle on the sill of the blind and put the crosshairs on it and discovered it to be a possum. He watched it eat along a few seconds, and then it did something really strange.

The possum raised his head and looked directly toward the blind and flashed the biggest grin that Mr. Pate said he'd ever beheld on anything other than a human. Looked like a mule might look grinning, he said, if mules grin. He picked up his binoculars, which he always carries with him hunting, and brought the beast into focus and discovered that the possum was indeed grinning and that his teeth looked like cow teeth. Then it went back to feeding.

Well, the old man was truly stumped. First of all, possums are not known for eating corn, though they will eat almost anything; second, this one had something other than regular possum teeth. His initial impulse was to shoot it so that he could examine it up close, but he couldn't do it, much as he hates possums. So he just watched it a little longer while he waited for a deer to show.

After it had finished the entree, the possum shambled over to the edge of the brush and began nibbling at some curly mesquite, which grows low and all over the place out there, like he was having salad. Now, the old man could understand a possum eating corn, but not curly mesquite. And then it started in on a clump of oats that had sprouted from seeds errantly flung during spring planting and ate them down to ground level. Mr. Pate wiped his eyes and the binocular lenses, but when he brought the glasses back up, the creature was gone.

He told Winship about the experience, and Winship told me, but neither of us put a whole lot of credence in the old man's observation. A possum with teeth like a cow, eating corn and curly mesquite and oats? We couldn't find anything in any book or on the internet that would suggest any possum would behave that way. So every time the subject came up, we just humored him and let the matter pass. But he knew that skepticism was running pretty high in both of us, and nothing would suit him but to take a picture of the thing or trap it so that we could see it for ourselves.

So here we are, standing before this wire trap looking down at the strangest creature I have ever seen. It is a full-grown, very large possum with a set of teeth like a cow, designed for chewing grass and grinding corn. We can't get it to grin, but when we act like we're going to attack it, it hisses, the way possums do, and when it does, it bares something that looks for all the world like a set of cow teeth.

"I call it the Nighturnal Remnant," Mr. Pate says, bringing his cigar back to life with a match.

"The what?"

"Well, Perfesser, you are a man of words. Winship too. What does *nighturnal* mean in your book?"

"He means *nocturnal*, Ruffin," Winship whispers. I'm not sure he has to whisper, since the old man can barely hear thunder, if he *does* hear it— probably just feels the vibration.

"It means of the night. In the case of a possum, a creature that roams and feeds at night."

"Arright then. And surely you know what a remnant is."

"Uh . . . ." Then Winship mouths *ruminant*.

"Yessir, it means basically that, like a cow, it eats grass and chews a cud."

"College has helped you out some then, I see." He takes a long drag on his cigar, blows a couple of rings, and turns to us.

"What say, fellers? Ain't that the damnedest thang you ever seen? Nothin' like that went up the gangplank of the ark. So the big question is, how did he get that way? His momma had to of crossed with a remnant."

I look at Winship, who shrugs, then say, "Possums are so ugly that it's a wonder their own *kind* are attracted to them, much less a goat or cow or sheep or deer. Besides, there's the physical problem involved. How in the world . . ."

"Beats me," Mr. Pate says. "I been shakin' my head over it ever since I first seen it. Not even a armadiller will court a possum, and they are the two ugliest beasts that Noah let on the boat. You get a mule by crossin' a jackass with a mare, but it's my understandin' that you gotta dig a hole for the mare to stand in for that to work. Now if some remnant was desperate enough to go for a possum, how would he do it? How would the possum get high enough for the remnant to reach the goodies? Get up on a stump? Been askin' myself over and over, and there ain't any answer that makes a lick of sense."

"What makes you think it didn't work the other way around?" I ask him. "What if the male was the possum?"

"Well, it seems to me that whut come out would of looked more like the remnant than the possum. Not much hair, though, and a long tail without hair. That awful lookin' face. But he'd be big and have hoofs."

"I . . ."

"Besides, wouldn't no remnant stand still for a ugly-ass possum hangin' on back there and doin' his bidness."

"There are all kinds of anatomical considerations here, guys."

"Nature works in mysterious ways," Winship says wisely. "I've heard of stumps being used by farm boys to reach *their* target, but I don't know about this." Then to the old man: "What're you going to do with him?"

"Turn him aloose, without some circus wants him. They's one comin' to San Antonio in late September, so I'll keep him fed until then and take him over there and see can I get a few bucks for him."

Later, back on the porch, we have a bowl of some kind of stew Mrs. Pate has whipped up—no way I'm going to ask what's in it, but it's good.

Then we talk possum a little while.

"I didn't know possums ranged this far west," I say to him.

"Well, they do. We ain't got as many as Missippi and East Texas, but we sure as hell *got*'m.

And they just as much trouble out here as they are back there. They been around as long as rocks." Mr. Pate is working on his third beer. "Most un-modern lookin' animal you can name—built like a Studebaker, with that pointy nose. Even their babies ain't cute, and you can't say that of anythang else's babies. You show me somebody that would cuddle one of them thangs and call it cute and I'll show you somebody that probably don't even like mayonnaise or meat."

Possums have been heavy on his mind since one fell down his chimney a few months ago and landed in a roaring fire, took on flame, and went skittering right across Mrs. Pate's wool rug, leaving a sooty trail that Mr. Pate said looked like "somebody had drug a burning log acrost it. And it one of them *imported* rugs at that. Imported from where? Arkansas, prolly. All's I know is that if it's got imported on the tag, it's gon' cost more than somethin' that ain't."

Now, lest any of you animal lovers out there become too concerned about the fate of the possum, Mrs. Pate put him out with a pan of dishwater and Mr. Pate put him farther out, into the yard, with a swift kick to his singed butt, more hairless than it was before he decided to play Santa Claus. They just today got a check from the insurance company, who finally relented and accepted the Pates' argument that though possums tumbling down the chimney and nearly burning up the house might not be specifically mentioned among the many hazards that might befall a homeowner, such things do, *by* God or in *spite* of God, happen and should therefore be covered. They have elected not to replace the rug, merely to give it a good shampooing, since if one possum did the dive, verily others might follow, a chickenwire guard currently in place notwithstanding.

He finishes his beer and reaches for another,

but Mrs. Pate, who's just walked onto the porch, smacks his hand and tells him that's enough, that he'll *rurn* his supper. I thought that the stew was supper, but I guess not.

"Ain't *no* redemption in a possum," he says, "which is why they've been around as long as dirt. Now, there was a time that people trapped them for their fur, which is a joke. Who the hell would wear anythang made out of possum hide?"

I shrug, and Mrs. Pate says, "I wouldn't. I know that. I ain't against fur, but I don't want no possum fur against me neither."

The old man looks longingly at the beer, which is propped up in a galvanized bucket of ice, while I'm still nursing my second. A six-pack between us a sitting is the usual, but he'll generally drink four and I'll have two. When Winship is along, there'll be two six-packs, and Mr. Pate will usually swill one down on his own. But it's his beer, after all.

"Most animals has got a hair count of somewhere around 1200 a square inch, which is more than you or me got." He rubs his almost-bald head. "Well, a hell of a lot more than me anyway. But a possum's got around forty a inch. You can actually count'm, they's so few of them. Which, as far as I am concerned, don't make it fur, just hide with a little bit of hair on it."

I study him a couple of seconds. "How do you know such stuff as this?"

"The internet," he says.

"Well," Mrs. Pate interrupts, "you can't knock the possum fur for the hair count because I heard tell that thin is in."

"They talkin' about women's bodies," he answers. Then he casts unkind eyes on Mrs. Pate's vast bulk, which has filled to overflowing the spring-legged lawn chair she's sitting in. "But I rekkin you ain't heard about that yet."

"This is in the genes and you know it, you

old fool," she says to him. "Momma was big, and you know that too. You just lucky you taken'n after your Daddy." She looks at me. "His Daddy left this world weighin' exactly a hunderd and twenty pounds more than he come in it with."

I decide to get the conversation back on track and dilute the tension that's beginning to build between them. "What else do you know about possums?"

He studies that one long enough that Mrs. Pate gets up and goes inside, and quicker than a snake-strike he has that beer uncapped and tilted and chugging. He lowers it. "They always go to the bathroom in the same place."

"What?" I lean forward in my chair.

"For a fact. Just like a goose choosin' a girl goose for life, possums choose a place to go to the bathroom—Number One, for sure—and that's where they always go."

"I never knew that."

"Never knew about the hair count neither, did you?" He waits for me to answer, but I don't. "Lotsa people think they got a roof leak, and then one day somebody crawls up in the attic and finds that a possum has chose that spot to do his bidness—Number One, that is. Number Two I ain't sure about. That's how come they don't ever travel far—gotta be able to get back to the spot ever three or four hours to pee. It's theirs for life." He hesitates, then: "By the way, they don't generally live but about three years, thank the Good Lord."

Well, I don't know how much the old man really knows about possums, and I don't care. I just know that if I were Noah and had to do some narrowing down of the cargo, the possum is one animal I'd direct into the bushes to drown. If that sounds cruel, I'm sorry. Life is, after all, pretty much a bitch.

We say our goodbyes and head on off to the

Rockpile. We're both pretty quiet on the way. Finally I say, "Bob, what we saw was real, wasn't it? I mean, the old man couldn't have doctored those teeth, could he?"

"I doubt it. No possum would hold still for that. Looked like the real thing to me. That possum had more and bigger teeth than the Pates put together."

I nod, keeping stride.

"By the way, if *she* is a remnant, I don't know that I want to see the whole thing."

I nod again.

Mrs. Pate on the Moon Walk

"The other day I was settin' out here thankin' about that colyum you done on the Mars Rover, I think they called it, the one to where you told about them takin' pitchers of Noah's ark up there."

"Yes'm." We're sitting on the front porch drinking coffee. If the old man were out here instead, it would be beer, but Mrs. Pate has never let a drop of alkyhawl, as she pronounces it, slip past her lips—knowingly, that is—except for beer. And she does not count cough medicines and other potions, like Hadacol (about fifty-proof), which she used to keep by the case in a closet. She now uses some more modern equivalent.

She fills to overflowing the metal lawn chair that she always sits in: once red with white arms and legs, but the paint's worn to bare metal in most places where her body touches it and it maintains a fair sheen from constant use. Little chance of rust.

We've also been talking about weight loss, a current enough issue for us both, since I could stand to shed a few pounds and she carries roughly twice the tonnage she'd like to—what my mother would have called stout (if she liked you), only Mrs. Pate evolved beyond stout many years ago. *Stout* is what the chair is that holds her up. But she says she's not willing to surrender foods that please her most—deer sausage and biscuits and real butter, bacon and potatoes and such—since, as she puts it, she'd rather be dead than not be able to eat them. She says what's the use of trying to go thin anyhow since the only purpose, so far as she sees, would be to try to attract another man, foolish enough since she already has one and *has* had him for over fifty years and he doesn't care what she looks like anymore, if he ever did. Love is blind, she says. I believe it. *Dead-ass* blind.

"Noah never lived on Mars," she continues. "I don't know what Rover—which is a dog's name, by the way, except I heard tell of a horse named that once—seen up there and take'n a pitcher of, but it wasn't no ark, at least not Noah's."

I shrug. "Well, it's just what I read about and reported. I doubt it too."

She reaches and picks up a log of deer sausage big as a rolling pin and cuts off a slice with a butcher knife and offers it to me, but I refuse, so she lays it on a cracker and slides the whole thing into her mouth. I'm figuring that the eight or ten teeth she's got in there, counting stalactites and stalagmites (and I'm not being unkind, because that's what Mr. Pate calls them too), will take a while with that rubbery sausage, but two chomps and it's down, chewed or not. She sips her coffee.

"And I don't care what they say—ain't nobody ever walked on that moon neither." She points her knife out over the fields toward the distant cliffs, where I can see the faintest ghost of a day moon standing on edge like a set of bull horns.

"Ma'am?"

"No sir. They done the whole thang in the desert somewhere out in Arizona, I heard tell. Done it in the dark and lit the place up like the sun was shinin' on it."

"But—"

"Lemme finish." She whacks off another slice of sausage, lays it on a cracker, and gives it the two-chomp motion, swallows, slurps her coffee like it's hot, but it's not.

"Did you know they's a cloud in the background of them pitchers they said they take'n up there? They tol' everbody it was just where they had dumped out the bathroom tanks where the asternauts had peed—excuse me for puttin' it like that, but it's what they said. Only thang is, experts that has studied that cloud says it looks to be a hunderd miles long. They couldn't of collected that much on the trip, even if they'd had beer along."

"A cloud of urine?"

"What they said, yeah, but it wasn't yurn—or theirs." She snickers at that.

"Tell you somethin' else. They squirted dust everwhere when they walked, which the experts says wouldn't happen, and when they jumped, they never got high enough to clear a hog layin' down. Shoulda been able to jump high as a man's head. Jumped just about as high as they would have in Arizona and raised just about as much dust."

"Well this—"

"They's more." She gives me a hard look, her eyes mere slits, her chin thrust out. "When they showed that on the television, that flag was wavin'. Couldn't do that on the moon, which ain't got wind—or so I been told—but it could do it in Arizona."

"I don't remember the flag waving—"

"Because one of them asternauts grabbed it and kept it still is how come. Then they tied it down or somethin'."

"I'm sorry, but—"

"They's a book out on it. Called *We Never Went to the Moon*. Guy named Bill somebody wrote it. I'm gon' get me a copy, and after I'm thoo with it you can read it."

"I'd appreciate that," I tell her.

Then she hoists herself out of the chair—which squawks, then sighs—and snatches up her sausage and crackers and lumbers into the house, letting the screen door slam behind her.

I sit around a few minutes waiting for her to come back out, but she doesn't, so I get up and step off the porch and head in the direction the old man went. About halfway across a patch of head-high mesquite, I stop and study the sliver of moon, pale and balanced delicately on end above the shimmering hills. "No," I say. "No way."

Mr. Pate Speaks of Shrinkwrop

It was the Christmas season, and I was out in San Antonio for a fiction panel at Barnes and Noble, so I decided I'd drive the extry (as Mr. Pate pronounces it) hour and a half west to jaw with my old friend, who has just turnt (Mrs. Pate's pronunciation) eighty.

Well, it may very well be the season to be jolly, with Sandy Claws poised to make his annual swoop down from the North Pole, but it is likewise the season for a whole lot of annoyances, not the least of which is shrinkwrap, that modern invention for protecting and preserving everything under the sun and driving nuts anybody trying to get through it.

We're sitting on the porch late in the day having Coronas—which Mr. Pate has switched to more or less full-time, someone having told him about a medical study touting the merits of Mexican beer, whether it's actually made and bottled in Mexico or not—and watching the great white cliffs drop into shadow. That river valley is beautiful anytime, but at sunup and sundown it is simply spectacular.

The old man has a big bandage on his thumb, so one of the first things I do is ask him about it, partly out of courtesy but mostly out of curiosity.

"Cut myself."

Now, some people might just right off ask, "How'd you manage that?" But I don't, because I know that just as sure as it will be dark in another hour, he is going to tell me every detail about how he cut that thumb—it's his nature.

See, Mr. Pate's not like the guy on the bus with three missing fingers (the guy, not the bus), which his fellow passenger is simply dying to ask him about. They ride along for a few blocks with the unmaimed passenger continuing to glance down where three fingers ought to be on a hand belonging to his next-seat neighbor. Got a thumb and little finger, but nothing in between. Finally he just has to ask, but he wants to be polite.

"Can I ask you a question?" he says to the guy with the missing fingers.

"I rekkin. As long as you ask just *one* question. That's all you get."

His neighbor points at the bad hand. "I just gotta know—how'd you lose them fingers."

The maimed guy says, "You mean them three fingers that ain't there?"

"Yeah," his neighbor says.

The guy holds his hand up like it's a trophy. "They got bit off." Now, he knows that the inquiring mind beside him knows that he can't ask another question, but he also knows that the guy will spend many a sleepless night wondering just *what* bit those fingers off, under what circumstances. I have never anyone yet with a body part missing that I didn't want to ask how that came to be. It's human nature.

Mr. Pate's not like the guy with the missing fingers. He likes to talk too much for that kind of foolishness.

The short of it is that he bought a power screwdriver over at a Sears store in San Antonio and when he couldn't worry the plastic wrap off of it, he take'n (as he put it) his pocket knife out and tried to cut his way in, in the process opening up his thumb the length it took five stitches to zip up.

"I just hate that stuff," he says, after he's finished his story. "Tougher than leather. And ever damned thang that you buy has got it on it. Buy a drill bit two inches long and a sixteenth of a inch in diameter and it'll come on a shrinkwropped card a foot long and six inches wide—I guess so it'll be harder to steal—that you can't get into to save your life without a knife. Bought one of them little ol' oven lightbulbs the other day and broke the damn bulb tryin' to get the plastic off of it. Next thang you know they'll be shrinkwroppin' eggs and you won't be able to get one out whole. I'm tellin' you . . ."

"You ever try to get a CD out of that stuff?"

"Naw. Got nothin' to play one in anyhow."

"Well don't, because only teenagers can do it in a reasonable length of time, and they have to use their teeth."

"I got to thinkin' one day about how the thang to do would be to have a little openin' tool with every package, but they'd shrinkwrop the tool too and you'd be no better off. Wear your fangernails to the quick tryin' to get the tool out to open the main package."

I laugh at that and we fish another Corona each out of the bucket he has them iced down in. The weather is fairly warm, and that beer feels good going down.

"You know," he on it again, "it looks to me like funeral home people would get in on the act. You know, instead of goin' thoo all that embalmin' stuff, they could just feed a corpse into a tube of shrinkwrap, seal the ends, then run'm thoo a little heat chamber and they'd come out lookin' just fine. Save everbody a heap of money. Lay'm out on a table for viewin' at the service and just put'm in the ground like that—wouldn't even need no coffin."

"Well, there's an idea, for sure," I say. "Let's talk it up with the Junction Funeral Home."

"'Nother thang I have thought about too—what if them Egyptians had of had shrinkwrop? They coulda saved all that cheesecloth and gauze or whatever the hell it was they used. Bet it take'n a whole acre of cotton to get enough mummy wrop to do up one of the them fay-rows."

"Did you ever see *Fried Green Tomatoes*?" I ask him. "I believe that was the movie. Anyway, in it a guy wrapped his wife with plastic wrap. Or maybe she did it to get his attention. I don't—"

He has just taken a swig of beer, which he spews all over the porch, he laughs so hard.

"Naw," he manages when he's gotten his breath back. "Ain't seen that, but me'n . . . ."

He drops his voice way low and nods toward the door. "Me'n her done that one time."

"You and—"

"Yep. I wropped her from her neck to her ankles. Big woman then too, so it take'n three whole rolls to do it right." He is giggling like a boy talking about seeing a girl naked for the first time, high-pitched and nervous.

"Once I got her wropped, I take'n the hairdryer to'r and tried to draw it up even tighter, but that stuff don't shrink from heat—only *I* didn't know that. Burnt her in four places before we realized that it was as tight as it was goin' to get. What the heat did do was glue that stuff together to where I thought I was gon' have to cut her out with my pocket knife."

"Well, Lord, Mr. Pate, common sense ought to tell you . . ."

"Common sense ain't got shit to do with most thangs that men try with women."

I nod at that.

The old man grumbles some more about shrinkwrap while he polishes off another beer, but his mood needle is beginning to swing a little higher.

Then Mrs. Pate's voice comes through the door: "Honey Bunch, see can you hep me with this—I need to whack up a chicken and my old ones are bad dull." She lumbers onto the porch and hands him a new set of kitchen shears, securely plastered to their cardboard backing with heavy-duty shrinkwrap.

He just sits there a few seconds staring at the shears, then hands them to me and fishes out his pocket knife.

"See'f you can get'm out without killing yerself. I don't want chicken that bad."

The Dark Truth about Marilyn Monroe

"Say *what?*" I look over at Mrs. Pate, who is shucking and silking a bushel basket of corn, which she will scrape off the cob and freeze later today. The sun is mid-morning high, and Mr. Pate is down on the river with Winship checking trotlines, leaving me on the porch with the old woman, who always insists that I listen to the latest news from her favorite tabloid, which she insists on calling a newspaper.

"At's right. Marilyn Monroe was a vampire and Ed Hoover had her kilt to keep her from bitin' JFK in the neck and turnin' *him* into one. It's a serious thang for a vampire to go gnawin' on the neck of the President of the Newnited States of America."

She refuses to call Hoover J. Edgar because she says people who use their first initial like that are uppity and because she says Edgar is an ugly name. She can't understand why he couldn't go by John, which was his first name. He's just Ed Hoover to her, only the way she says it makes it sound like he never did anything more important than invent a vacuum cleaner.

"And I take it that was in the—uh, your— newspaper?"

"Right back there in the bafroom in a basket by the commode. You want me to get it for you?"

"No, thank you." I'm having a glass of iced tea

while I prepare myself for this news about Marilyn.

"She was bit back in 1950 by a movie director that seducted her at a party. She wasn't nuthin' until she got converted to a vampire, and then she take'n off like a rocketship. Wudn't no time at all till the whole world knowed about her—not about her bein' a vampire, about her bein' a hot-shot movie star. How come she wore so much makeup, you know, to where she could go out in the daylight like a ordinary person."

"What did makeup have to do with it?"

"She wore it real thick, and it had sun block in it. Vampires can't take the sun, you know. Does somethin' bad to'm. Hives maybe. I don't know."

"Who all knew about it? About her being a vampire?"

"Well, some folks did, all I know. Joe what's his name, the baseball player she married, he fount out about it and dumped her. Word is that he take'n a baseball bat and whittled it into a stake and was gon' run it thoo her but backed out. Some of the people that worked for her knew too, because she fahred a cook that put garlic in her food one time and a gardener that wore a crux . . . you know, a . . . a crossifix or whatever they're called. Little cross with Jesus on it.

"She was all the time lettin' fans get in her limousine and latchin' her fangs in they necks and suckin'm dry. Didn't nobody know this till the article come out, but she bit Clark Gable, which is why he had a heart attack and died when he did."

"Aw, come on, Mrs. Pate . . . ."

"It is the God's honest truth, Perfesser. It is in the newspaper."

"Yeah, well . . . ."

"Ed Hoover was trackin' her the whole time, tapped her phones and everthang, so he was in on what she was doin'. It was when she started messin' around with JFK that he decided he had to do somethin' about her, and he had her kilt."

"What'd he do, drive a stake through her heart?" I figure I might as well play along, since I'm caught up in it anyway.

"Naw, he had his FBI boys take care of her. Couldn't use no stake. That would be too obvious."

"So . . . ."

"His agents broke into her place and shot her up with holy water, which fried her organs from the inside. Whut the corner said. He said her canine teef was real long and that she had blood in her mouth that didn't match hers. Said her body was just slathered with that sun block, might near a quarter of a inch thick. And here's the kicker: She had hairs on the palms of her hands and her fangernails was unnatural, they was so long."

"Hair on her palms?" I always heard that only one thing did that to you, but I figure I'd better not bring that up.

"All that's factual. It's in the newspaper. Yon't me to go get it? I know right where it's at. Right by the commode."

"No, ma'am. I'll take your word for it."

"Been lots of other Hollywood stars was vampires too. James Dean and Rock Hudson. Matter a' fact, it was James Dean bit Rock Hudson on the set of *Giant* and later got AIDS from suckin' blood."

"Dean did?"

"Naw, Rock did. Dean was kilt in a car wreck. He was drivin' a Porch or somethin' like that. One of them fast farn cars."

"What other vampires were there, *are* there?"

"I don't know, except for what the newspaper says. Cary Grant was, and Gretter Garbo. Rudolph Valentine was too."

"Valentino," I correct her.

"Whatever," she says, going at her corn.

I can see Mr. Pate's truck inching up the drive now, so I get up and start out to meet them, see what they caught.

"If you got time later, Perfesser," she says just before I'm out of hearing, "I'll tell you about how it was a Jap submarine sunk the *Titanic*, not no iceberg."

I stop and turn around and think about saying something, but she's really getting into that corn now, and I don't exactly know where I'd begin.

Mr. Pate and the Draft

It's yet another late afternoon on Mr. Pate's front porch, and Winship and the old man and I are drinking from tall glasses of tea so packed with ice that there's probably not much more than a cup of tea in them. The air's so dry that the glasses barely sweat.

Mr. Pate's grousing over the fact that he's been trying with little success to talk one of his great-grandsons into joining the Air Force or Navy for some training in electronics—and for some discipline. The boy told him, "Hey, Mr. Custer, I don't wanna go," echoing the lyrics from a song popular a few decades ago—you remember it, with drums beating in the background and Indians whooping. Ray Stevens, I think. The boy doesn't want to give up whatever freedom he's got for even less, so he's dug in his heels and declared flatly that they might burn the woods and tote out his ashes, but he is not going to join any branch of the Armed Forces as long as he has the resources to resist.

"It's not a popular thing, joining the military these days," Winship says.

"Never was terribly popular," I add.

The old man snorts. "I joined. And they was a war on then too, and a real big one. And I actually got close enough to the action in North Africa that one day a piece of shrapnel dented my helmet."

I report to them: "I was reading the other day that the Army, Air Force, and Navy are all anticipating shortfalls in recruitment over the next year."

Winship snorts. "Why would a kid knocking down fairly good money, enough at least to consider himself fairly independent, go off into the military for a disciplined life and for what, even these days, is paltry pay?"

I turn to him and smile. "Well, it's better than the $87 a month I earned."

"And I didn't make even half that," Mr. Pate says.

We are silent for awhile, watching the little herd of Black Buck Antelope Mr. Pate has put together run from my son, who's chasing them in a pen just a bit bigger than a football field. They whirl together in formation, tight and coordinated, leap high in the air, like spring-loaded toys, dividing around the boy, then closing on the other side into their formation again.

"That boy'll never get near one of'm."

"No sir," I say, "but at least he'll wear down a bit trying, burn off some energy."

"Won't wear *them* down, though. I 'spect they think it's a game."

"Yessir, they do," Winship says. "And they like it because they're winning."

The old man rares back in his chair and says sagely, "Because they was born to run from thangs that tries to catch'm. Nature's disciplined them that way."

Before I can stop myself, I break out with a couple of lines from the poet Robinson Jeffers: "What but the wolf's tooth whittled so fine the fleet limbs of the antelope?"

"I don't get it," the old man says. "What's a wolf's tooth got to do with a antelope's limbs? I guess he means legs and feet. And by *fleet* he means *fast*. Am I close?"

"Right on," I say.

"But what does a wolf's tooth—"

"It's poetry, Mr. Pate. It's not supposed to mean anything to normal people."

"Thanks, Winship," I say.

There's silence again as we watch the boy angle across the patch for another attack on the antelope, who've gathered in a clump behind a line of low mesquite, their little heads darting and dodging as they stand watching.

Mr. Pate finally speaks. "You know, I was thankin' the other day that it sure would be good if they brought back the draft."

We all study on this a minute, and he continues. "The kids we got comin' along these days—the boys that is—don't have no respect for authority or discipline, got no sense of responsibility, don't have no direction in life. The military'd give'm all that." He took a draw off his tea. "I was a smartmouth punk of a boy when I went in, but basic trainin' straightened me out. I had a sergeant made a believer out of me."

"I did too," I say. "A master sergeant snatched me up by the lapels of my fatigue jacket one day and slammed me against the barracks wall and advised me that he wasn't going to take that kinda talk from me—I can't imagine what I said to him or how I said it, but you'd better believe that I chose my words very carefully after that."

The old man laughs. "One kicked my butt, hard. That was back when they could do it and not have to go to sensitivity trainin' to get their heads straightened out afterwards. By the time I got out of the Army I knew what authority was, and I knew how to talk to my superiors with respect—I learned I *had* superiors—and I knew how to make up a bed and keep my own clothes clean and in order . . ."

"The military *used* to do that. I don't know whether it does anymore or not."

He looks at me. "But it'd sure hell help. Take these little smartmouths just brimmin' with testy-rone and send'm off for a year with Army sergeants as their mommas and teachers, and they'd come back here with a different attitude. I say take'm the day after they cross the high school stage and send'm off for a year of active duty. Some European countries do it, and it works out fine. And if they're troublemakers, send'm off even before they graduate. Then let'm come back and get jobs or go to college. You'd have a lot less trouble with them. That I'd guarantee. The Army'll wear'm down, discipline'm, take all that—" He notices his wife out of the corner of his eye. "All that piss and vinegar out of'm."

"Subdue them to the useful and the good," Winship says, echoing Tennyson.

"That'd be one way of puttin' it," says the old man.

The boy's wearied now and started out of the pen, while the antelope eye him, bending their necks this way and that, almost like they're sorry he's leaving. And maybe they are.

We surrender our empty glasses to Mrs. Pate and head off down the road toward Winship's place, three abreast, our feet falling in unison, the boy having to stretch but keeping cadence—right, left, right, left, right, left, right . . . .

Amelia Earhart and Other News

"Thunder Beans?" I have shifted in my chair so that I can look into Mrs. Pate's face. She's just told me that Thunder Beans brought down Amelia Earhart's Lockheed Electra back there in July of 1937, when she finally lost radio contact with the Coast Guard cutter *Itasca* somewhere in the vicinity of Howland Island in the Pacific and fell into the regions of myth.

"New Ginny Thunder Beans is what the newspaper says. I've got the article right there in the bafroom, if you want me to go get it. I cut it out to put in my scrapbook."

"No ma'am, that won't be necessary, but I would like to hear about this new theory." I mean, who wouldn't? Amelia's disappearance is one of the greatest mysteries ever.

"Arright, here's the scoop on it, as they say in the newspaper binness." She shifts her massive body in the lawn chair she's couched in and points up. "They was flyin' across the globe, which is what people sometimes call the world, her and this guy name Noonan, who was sposed to be tellin' her where they was at at any perculiar time, and I rekkin he had been doin' a purty fair job of it, since he got'm to a place called Lay, or somethin' like that, in New Ginny. That island they was sposed to land on was over two thousand miles away, so they decided they would eat plenty for that long trip, which they done, only Ameelyer, she eat two bowls of what they call Thunder Beans in New Ginny."

"Why Thunder Beans?" I ask her.

"Well, it ain't like they could lay in some Big Macs." She slides a foot out of one of her slippers and examines the big toe, then holsters it again.

"Now, they was sposed to land on that island, to where they could get gas from that Coast Guard boat that was lazin' around the edge of it. And they got close enough to get in radio contact with the boat, only after a while they lost the signal and ain't nobody ever heard of'm again. Nothin' but static was what they heard on that boat after Ameelyer told'm she was runnin' low on gas."

The old woman smiles knowingly, then resumes: "Now's where them Thunder Beans come in. See, they are real bad about givin' people the gas, which is where their name comes from. A few hours after you eat'm, they start to work on you, and that's what they done to Ameelyer."

I am not believing what I am hearing.

"They was some notes that they found that the guy Noonan wrote, and he describes how that it was so bad in the plane that they was both hangin' their heads out the winders. And one of his notes says that she couldn't keep'r head inside the plane long enough to read her instruments and then that they was goin' down."

"*What* notes?" I ask her.

"The notes that they found in the travel bag."

I'm agitated now. "*What* travel bag? If they went down, where did the notes and the travel bag come from?"

"Ain't sayin' they crashed, only that they went down. They might of landed on another island or somethin'. Or maybe the bag fell out of the plane. I am just tellin' you what the newspaper says. Somebody found the notes and the travel bag, and they done them tests on the stuff and decided that it blonged to Ameelyer and Noonan."

"Tests?"

"You know, the *DN*-sumthin' or other tests."

"What kind of DNA samples could they get—"

"Yon't me to go get the article for you?"

I raise my hands. "No ma'am. I'll take your word for it."

"Some other good stuff in there too," she says. "Like there's this guy that has caught the Toofairy and has got her in a cage, like a bird. The guy that caught her says she's about the size of his fanger. He baited a trap with two teef and caught her."

I want to laugh, but she's so serious that I dare not. "Now, why would anybody want to go and catch the Tooth Fairy and put her in a cage?"

"To find out where she gets her money at and what she does wif all them teef. I mean, ain't you wondered about that yerself, Perfesser? She been pickin' up teef from under pillers forever. Ain't you ever wondered where she gets all them quarters at and what does she do wif the teef?"

"Uh, no'm, I really haven't."

"Well, I sure wanna know. He's gon' torture her until she spills the beans." She cackles at that, but I am fairly unamused.

"They got a airysawl spray now that you can use to get rid of ghosts and demons. Zaps'm just like bugs."

"I—"

"And you wouldn't bleeve it, but that A-rab television network, Al Jazeery, or whatever it's called, they gon' have a show like *Friends*, only they gon' call it *BagDad Buddies*. They a bunch of messed-up people settin' around plottin' mischief. They even gon' try to brang in some American act-ers to star in it. Gonna try to get Bill Clinton to play a door-to-door gun salesman, peddlin' KA-74 rifles."

"That would be AK-47s, I suspect."

"Whatever. It'd be sumthin' if they got him. Even got a spot for the real Osommer . . ."

"Osama?"

"Yep. It's gon' be a real popler show, I figger."

"I'll bet it will be."

"You want some tips on how to survive in Hell?"

"Well, Mrs. Pate, I'm not sure . . . . Uh, OK, how *do* you survive in Hell?"

"The main thang is that you don't want to sass the demons in charge down there, not if you want good food and want to get treated right."

There usually comes a point when I'm listening to her and that tabloid stuff that I feel like a jar that has been filled completely up to the rim and one more drop will send me over the edge. I've reached it. I simply cannot take another drop. So I stand and stretch and thank her for the tea and tabloid news and head off down the road to the Winship place.

You ever tried walking along a road with your head focused on nothing whatsoever? Well, it can be done.

Pulling in His Financial Horns

"Because it costs too damned much to *run* it is how come."

Bob Winship and I are sitting on Mr. Pate's front porch in the dead of August, sweltering, with not so much as a feather wisp of breeze blowing, but as Winship has pointed out, the high desert climate is bearable even in the heat of the most savage days of summer.

"It's a dry heat," Mr. Pate has told me so many times that I no longer say, "So's that in Hell." I just nod and continue to bake. Sweat doesn't have a chance to bead before it's sucked up by air that feels like what you feel when you open the oven door to see whether the cornbread's done.

Mr. Pate is explaining to me and Winship why he no longer uses his central system during the day. It's one thing out here to throw the windows open at night and maybe use a ceiling fan—it's another to fool with this heat in the daytime.

I mean, I grew up in Mississippi without air conditioning, but once I experienced it, I never wanted to be without it again.

"The 'lectric bill has done got to the point that we gotta start shavin' back the budget. Me'n the lady was brought up in this country without air conditionin', and it ain't a bit hotter now than it was then, no matter what they say about global warmin'. So the A/C is one of the first thangs to go. We can live without it. I just wish we had never got the A/C to begin with, since if you ain't never had it, you can't miss it. Know what I mean? Used to drive around with the winders in the car down in the summertime. Didn't nobody complain—because they had never had the A/C."

Like most of us, the Pates have had to come to terms with the hard realities of an economy in which what money you have managed to put aside earns in dividends right at a tenth of what it earned a few years ago. Utilities keep going up, right along with taxes and insurance, because you have to have all three and because there's not much dealing you can do, except maybe shop around a little to save pennies on insurance rates, but the money to manage our home budgets is coming from a smaller and smaller stream. As the old man so aptly put it when Winship and I mentioned the metaphor, "That stream is fast turnin' into a trickle. Purty soon there won't be anythang but little mudholes we'll be dippin' out of."

Once he dabbled a little bit in the market, but now he's afraid to commit anything to something as "wishy-washy as the weather," preferring to keep his money in CDs and regular savings accounts. A few months ago while we were sitting out here, he pointed to a spider thread that stretched from the doorway out to the end of one of the porch rafters.

"You see how that thread moves with the breeze, driftin' this way and that?"

We nodded.

"Well that is just what the stock market is. It is a spider thread that is moved by every chanch breeze. And you do you know what it would take to break it? Absolutely nothin'. Let a bug hit it, or a humminbird, or the old lady's broom, or let the wind pick up, and that thang's broke half in two."

We just kept nodding.

"Now I am tellin' you this from common sense, which means that I can perdict the market as well as all them people writin' articles about it. They can't predict that market as well as the weather people do the weather, because even the weather people know it sure as hell ain't gon' frost in Segovia, Texas, in July or August. Anythang can happen to snap that thread up there."

What he said made sense that day.

They've given up Mrs. Pate's ten-year-old Camry, which they never used for anything but going to church on Sunday anyway. Not much of a savings, he says, but it helps. Their Toyota Tacoma, nearly six years old but in super shape, is their only transportation. With four-wheel drive, it will go anywhere in any kind of weather, and after Mrs. Pate finally came to the realization that friends were giving up *their* sedans too, relying totally on pickups to get around, she took it with better spirits.

"We had planned a trip over to North Careliner to visit some in the fall, but it ain't gonna happen, not with gas prices what they are and motels to have to stay in and expensive restrunt food. Gonna ride it out here, where at least we got catfish in the river and more deers than you can shake a stick at. Got cows. Could get pigs. And we can grow a right smart of stuff out here when we irrigate. Used to run a pipe up from the river and irrigate twenty acres out there." He points out behind the house. "I can still do that."

They have begun to eat lighter now and turned more to cheap canned foods: vegetables and Spam and soups and such. Once in a while they'll treat themselves to a trip to the Segovia Truck Stop for Western omelets and biscuits or maybe chicken-fried steak on Friday nights.

"Let me tell you, boys," he says, sipping on his tea. "We in a death spiral here. People don't seem to reconize it, from Warshington down to the ranch, but we got worse times comin'."

"How bad do you figger?" I ask him, more to keep him talking than anything else. I love to hear him talk.

"Well, look. Most retired people was doin' OK when their dividends was runnin' right at seven percent. They had money to buy extry thangs with. Bought a new car ever few years. Didn't like the risin' insurance and utility bills and taxes, but their budgets could handle'm. What they gonna buy extries with now? How they gonna balance they budgets when they makin' a tenth on their money to what they was makin' three years ago? Social Security sure as the hell won't keep'm afloat. They dippin' into savings is how, which can't last forever.

"And you got people bein' laid off right and left and freezes on hahrin' and budget cuts right down the line. State budgets in a mess. And them that's workin' ain't gon' get raises or bonuses."

"Pretty negative stuff, Mr. Pate."

"You can bet on it, Perfesser. And it's gon' get negativer."

He takes another sip of tea. "So that's how come my lady is settin' in front of a fan, lettin' it blow up her dress, instead of enjoying the comforts of air conditionin'."

A few silent minutes later Winship and I say good-bye and start off on back to the Rockpile.

"Are things as bad for them as he's letting on, Bob?" I ask him.

"Oh yeah. See, they sold off pieces of their land to build a retirements nest egg. Had right at half a million dollars stashed in those high-yielding CDs. Must have been making nearly $40,000 a year over Social Security. Now they're lucky to clear five or six grand. Yeah, they're hurting."

We walk on for a while in silence, our shoes scuffing the caliche.

"Do you think things are as bad all over as he does?"

Winship stops and looks toward the great cliff the sun has just slid over.

"Oh, yeah, I do, I do."

Ah, but the evening is pleasant, and we have Shirley's fantastic Mexican casserole awaiting us back at the ranch, and neither of us wants to talk anymore about the economy. Sometimes a nice walk and anticipation of good food and a little wine is what contentment comes down to.

Summer Sausage

"What exactly *is* this?" I ask Mrs. Pate as she hands me a small platter with saltines and several slices of something that looks vaguely like summer sausage. "Summer sausage?"

She shuffles back to her lawn chair and wallows down into it like something intent on making a nest and raising young. It is mid-afternoon, hot already, though it is early April.

"Lord, naw," she says. "Ain't no way I'd put summer sausage before nobody. That stuff ain't comin' in this house."

She hesitates, then: "How come they call that stuff summer sausage anyhow? You can eat it any day of the year—if you was desprit enough *to* eat it. Never understood how it got its name."

She points to the tray. "At's Axis sausage, made out of Axis deer meat and chunks of pork, with plenty of spices. Got a man in Junction grinds it up and packages it for us. It's good. Go on and try it out."

So I do, and she's right: It *is* good. Just salty enough, just spicy enough. Axis meat is like beef anyway, so it's hard to go wrong with it.

"What do you have against summer sausage?"

Now, I know better than to open the door on this kind of thing. I've been coming out here long enough to know that Mr. and Mrs. Pate are set in their ways and their ways are like concrete, or con*creek*, as she would put it. Whatever they believe, they believe resolutely, and not the Almighty Himself could change them. But I love to hear her get off on her tangents, whether what she says makes a lick of sense or not. About the time she gets primed to answer, Winship and Mr. Pate come onto the porch and take a seat.

"What I got against it is what all they put in it." She slides a cracker, piggy-backed with a slice of Axis sausage, into her mouth and goes at it with the few teeth she has left. She has a couple of partials in a drawer somewhere that fill her out, as she puts it, but she says they're too much trouble, except on Sundays, when she wears them to smile at church.

"You name it and it come off a cow or a pig, and it is in there. Everthang you or me'd thowe away if we was butcherin'. Got stomach, guts, lungs, spleen, kidneys, brain, liver, bones, blood, eyeballs . . ."

"Eyeballs?"

"Why wouldn't they thowe eyeballs into the pot, Perfesser? They bulk too, and once they ground up, you can't tell they're in there."

"Gums and adenoids, eyelids, gallbladders and sinuses and mucous membrane, too, I heard tell." The old man is in on it now.

Winship is loving it. "How about hair and hooves, teeth, and horns?"

Mrs. Pate slings her jowls back and forth. "Naw, 'cause people would spot hair or pieces of teef and hoofs. You can't grind them fine enough. Too hard. People'd bite down on a chunk of somethin' like that and break a toof and want to sue."

She leans forward in her chair. It groans and complains but holds steady as a trestle. "Y'ever read the labels on stuff like summer sausage and potted meat and Vienna sausage, stuff like that?"

I shake my head no.

"Well, y'ort to sometime. It will open your eyes."

"And shut down your hunger," Winship adds.

She settles back in her chair again and pontificates: "They got fancy little cover-up words like *meat by-products*, you know. And that means that it ain't meat. It is what kept the meat alive and held it together and up walkin' around until it ended up dead. It's all them thangs I mentioned, and prolly a lot more that I didn't."

"You forgot about that term *mechanically separated poultry* that they use on them labels too," Mr. Pate says.

"What the hell does that mean?"

"I'll tell you whut it means, Perfesser," the old woman breaks in. "It means what they do is take chicken bones and tissure that ain't used in any other way and grind it up and force it thoo a sieve and they come up with a kinda paste that goes to bulk up stuff like potted meat and summer sausage is whut it means."

I keep staring at the slices of Axis sausage on my plate. Once this conversation got really rolling, I just nibbled at my crackers. Right now I am in no mood for *anything* to eat.

"Partially defatted cooked pork fatty tissure, partially defatted cooked beef fatty tissure, stuff like that, that don't tell you nothin'. All that does is confuse me." The old lady is animated now.

Winship laughs out loud. "And don't forget sodium erythorbate, dextrose, sodium nitrate, sodium nitrite, corn syrup, lactic acid, hydrolyzed corn gluten, wheat gluten proteins, water, and Lord knows what other little dribblings to do this and that to keep it marginally fit for human consumption and give it extra shelf life"

"Give me a chunk of head cheese any day," Mr. Pate says.

I spin around and look at him. "What? That sounds disgusting, about as appetizing as ear wax or toe cheese."

"Y'ain't heard of head cheese?"

"Yes, I heard about it growing up, but I never developed a whole lot of curiosity about it."

"Made out of the head meat off a pig," he says.

Winship now takes the floor, so to speak. Having been to medical school and all, he knows a great deal more about most things than the average person. "What they do is clean the head and boil it until all the meat falls off the bone. Then they take the meat and chop it up, sometimes with other parts of the pig, and season it and put it back in the water it was boiled in. They pour it into molds and chill it, and what comes out is a jellied loaf that can be sliced. I don't eat it myself, but Mr. Pate finds it a delicacy."

Like Scarlett in the garden, I lift my eyes to the heavens and declare, "As God is my witness, I will never be hungry again."

"Aw, Perfesser, we talkin' about stuff you buy in the store." She points to my plate. "At sausage there ain't got nothin' but Axis deer meat and the best cuts of hog meat in it. I don't even take a chanch of it goin' bad just layin' around—I freeze it right off. I unthawed that just this mornin'."

"Unthawed it?"

"Just this mornin'."

I stand up. "Uh, Bob, I guess we'd better be going, don't you think? I wanted to hunt a little while this afternoon." What I mainly want to do is not burst out loud laughing. You know that feeling you used to get in church as a kid, like you know one more goofy-ass thing said from the pulpit and you're going to just lose it . . . .

He nods and rises and we say our goodbyes.

"She *unthawed* it just this mornin', Bob," I mutter as we walk along the caliche road toward home, our feet making little whispering sounds, and then we don't talk for a long time. When we do, it is not about food.

Mr. Pate Spices Up His Love Life

We're sitting on the porch, late. The sun has just finished another day of beating up on the landscape and gone home over the hills, leaving the valley bruised with evening purple. We've been just jawing some, mostly about what kind of deer have been taken out of the valley lately and what kind of yield folks are getting from their trotlines on the river. Winship looks around to make certain Mrs. Pate is not within hearing distance of the porch and says to me, quietly and on the old man's bad-ear side, "Get him to tell you about trying Viagra."

"Viagra?"

"Yeah, ask him about it."

So I do. I say, "Mr. Pate, Bob tells me you've tried the new drug—you know, the little blue pill, Viagra."

He leans forward in his chair and smiles at us. "Sure did. Hell of a boost to a man's drive, you know. Does the job." He gives me a shrewd look. "Made me feel like a pube again, with slicked-back hair and tight pants and a tee-shirt with the arms tore off, ready to take on the whole cheerleadin' team."

"That good, huh?"

"I'll say." He scoots his chair closer to mine and lowers his voice. "Gon' let you in on somethin', though, that most folks don't know about." His eyes grow shrewd again. "There's a cheaper version than the pills. Them thangs cost ten dollars apiece. I use the powder."

I glance at Winship, who gives me a knowing wink, then to the old man. "Uh, I didn't know it came in powder form."

"More granular, I'd say," Winship puts in.

"Yeah, granular maybe," Mr. Pate agrees. "Whatever, you just mix a teaspoon of it in a medium-size glass of water and slug it down. Tastes purty bad, but it's a hell of a lot cheaper than the pill."

I say to Winship, "Bob, I don't follow this. I haven't heard about a granular form of Viagra."

Mr. Pate beams again. "Been around for years too. Folks just didn't know about this perticlar use for it."

"See, Ruffin," Winship says, "Mr. Pate gets his potion at the feedstore."

I look at Bob, then at the old man. "Come on, guys, what gives here? You can't get Viagra at a feedstore. It's by prescription. And I don't think it comes in granular form either."

"You'd be sprised what you can get at a feedstore. They don't tell you everthang in the news. If it got out about this cheaper version, there'd be a run on it."

"Winship, do you know what he's talking about?"

Bob grins. "Show him the stuff, Mr. Pate."

The old man rises from his chair and shuffles off into the house. In less than a minute he's back with a little green box, which he hands me. "There y'are. The real stuff. And it ain't but $5.95 for enough to last a man weeks, or months if he's slown down much—well, maybe a year if he's slown down a lot. And you can get five pounds of it for around fifteen bucks."

"You didn't tell him about the side-effects, Mr. Pate," Winship says.

The old man spits into a coffee can and wipes the corners of his mouth with his hand. "It's blue too, like the pill, so it gives you a blue tongue, for one thang. And a monstrous headache that makes you feel like your skull is splittin' wide open. Indigestion too, if you take it on a empty stomach." He cackles and slaps his leg. "But it's worth it, I'm tellin' you, worth it!"

The first stars are blazing away as Winship and I start off to his place. The road dust, hanging deadwind from the last passing truck, has coated the shrubs and trees, and they look white and ghostly. The only sound is the whizzing of faraway traffic on the interstate, our shoes crunching on caliche, and the bark of an axis buck down in the river bottom.

I say finally, "Bob, Mr. Pate's using plant food for—."

"Yep. Viagro. Been around for years."

"Same color as Peters' Plant Food. Bob, you've got a medical background. Do you think it really does anything for him?"

"Perhaps something from the nitrates? I don't know. Might irritate his urinary tract enough to get something going. If he *thinks* it does, though, then it probably does. The placebo effect is a strong one."

"It won't hurt him?"

"Probably not. Just the blue tongue and the headaches, occasional indigestion. But to him it's worth it."

"Mercy," I say.

"Sir?"

"Suppose he starts growing too, gets younger? Wouldn't that be something?"

"Who's to say? We'll study him. If it happens, we'll know where to put our money."

The People and the Land

The Cowbirdboys of Segovia

The cage we are standing before is big enough to hold anything up to a small black rhino, measuring some eight-by-five feet and standing a good seven feet high, made of angle iron and wire mesh (the cage, not the theoretical rhino). It is situated in a stand of mesquite several hundred feet from the Winship house. I've seen hog traps out here, but they aren't nearly this big. And this one has a door that a man can walk through, but it's latched, which means that even if a small rhino or Russian Boar did decide to go in there, he'd have to figure out how to remove the clevis pin first.

But let me back up a little. I'm looking at this thing with Bob Winship, Mr. Pate, and Barbara Holland Criswell, who has come all the way from Mississippi to visit Winship's Rockpile Ranch, which I've talked and written so much about that she had to satisfy herself that it exists, and to meet Mr. Pate, whom she figured I just made up. Barbara's my mentor's daughter, and I've known her since she was a teenager, and she's a dear family friend, but she has this cynical edge to her . . . . My son is off on the river somewhere, and Shirley, who is not at all impressed with the birds or cage or the two men running it, is working on supper.

The big cage is all aflutter with small black birds with brown heads. I have counted right at twenty-five of them, but they are fluttering all over the place, so a precise count is pretty difficult. Let's just say that there are a couple of dozen in it. They are male cowbirds, Barbara and I have been told. Since she's an Audubonner, she didn't have to be told, but I did. They are in the cage to attract female cowbirds, which are a little duller in color (what a nice rhyme) than the males but not in intellect, which accounts for the fact that there are only males in the cage. There is a human analogy at work here, but I won't push it. I'll just say that cages come in all sizes.

But I have to back up again here. Bob and Mr. Pate are participating in a State program designed to diminish the population of cowbirds, a parasitic creature that lays its eggs in the nests of nicer birds, after kicking the other birds' eggs out. The indigenous females, being gentle and maternal, as the females of any species generally are, unless some sorry-ass male has turned them sour, go on and hatch the cowbird eggs and raise the young and simply add to the cowbird population. So far as I know, nothing has been written on the reaction of the local daddies, who must surely from time to time wonder about the oddballs who hatch out with the others. I can imagine one shaking his head and thinking, *Well, damn, them four don't look a thing like either one of us.*

These creatures became major players on the bird scene during the great buffalo migrations of a century and a half ago, following the buffalo and laying their eggs wherever they could in the nests of the local birds and moving on, Nature having designed them so. The buffalo disappeared, but not the cowbirds, since they were not nearly as succulent a target as the buffalo were to hunters—I mean, who'd be interested in cowbird hides or tongues? The buffalo are largely gone, but the cowbirds have done throve, as Mr. Pate puts it. I doubt that buffalo hunters were part of Nature's plan.

The upshot is that the State, urged by the Federal Guvmint, has come up with a program whereby ranchers in West Texas might curtail the cowbird scourge by trapping as many females as possible and eradicating them, thereby protecting the local species, over 200 varieties. It's part of a complex agricultural tax-exemption plan for the land. According to State statistics, in unprotected areas the rate of parasitism (the percentage of cowbird hatchlings as opposed to indigenous hatchlings) is roughly 80%, but where traps are employed, that rate drops to around 20%. So the plan works pretty well.

Now, Barbara's as rabid a bird sympathizer as you're likely to find, so she's reeling from all this, but she agrees with her late momma that the cowbird is a *bad bird* and deserving of death, at the very least. Eternal damnation would be more suitable, but I'm not sure there *is* a hell for birds. Her attitude is simply that if by knocking off cowbirds you are saving songbirds, she's all for it. She's a feminist, too, but a reasonable one, believing, as she does, that males serve a purpose beyond mere seed dissemination—in this case enticing female cowbirds into the trap.

Well, the question just necessarily arises that if you are trapping female cowbirds, what the hell do you do with them once you have them in the cage? And what to do with the extra males?

Winship wonders just why any female cowbird would enter a cage with two dozen horny males anyway, but Mr. Pate points out that at least there's food in there and water and free lodging, so why wouldn't she, which makes sense to me, though again I am perplexed by the fact that there are no females in the cage. It is strange territory for me, and I don't mean this marvelous river valley.

Finally I ask again, "OK, guys, once you catch the females, what do you do with them?"

"We have to dispatch them," Mr. Pate says.

"You *kill* them?" Barbara asks.

"For a fact," Mr. Pate says.

"And do what with them?" I ask.

Winship shrugs. "Well, I catch mine with a net and clip their heads off with a pair of shears and feed them to my cats."

The old man wags his head. "Not me. I foller the State's instructions and wring they necks. The instructions say to hold them by the neck with your thumb and forefinger and to pull and twist until you feel them little neck bones give. When the head flops over, they are dead. Like they gotta tell you that. If the head flops over, what do you figger, that they just dozed off? After they quit moving for several minutes and I am sure they ain't got enough life left in'm to fly off, I take'm home and freeze'm for cookin'."

"Blackbird pie, huh?" I ask him.

"For a fact," he says.

OK, things are getting surreal, but I'm game, so I just ask, "And precisely what does a cowbird taste like?"

Mr. Pate studies the question a few seconds. "Kinda like chicken," he says.

"What *doesn't?*" Barbara asks, ready to head back down the path toward civilization, toward wine and supper.

"Hey, Perfesser," he says to me, "you remember that casserole you had over at our place earlier in the sprang, that *chicken* casserole that you liked so much?"

He does not have to finish. I am way ahead of him. I've also decided to catch up to Barbara and let the cowbirdboys do their thing.

"You think he was joking?" I ask her.

"Don't know. You've eaten crow a few times."

"Yeah, but I sure didn't enjoy it. That casserole was fantastic. I can't believe . . . ."

"You wouldn't be the first person to eat cowbird," she says.

I'll tell you, there are times out here that you just don't know what's on your plate, whether it once flew or walked or swam or just lay around. I whisper to Barbara to be quiet as we slip into Shirley's kitchen—I want to know what's coming for supper.

Making a Dam in Segovia

Winship and I are standing on the bank above the Johnson Fork of the Llano, which cuts across the corner of his property on its way north to the Colorado.

"Guidry [that's Mike Guidry, out from Houston, who lays claim to one of Bob's hunters' cabins] put in a trotline last night, and he said the river's silted in. But it's not that." He points to the rock dam that arches two-thirds of the way across to a tapering shoal. "The dam's got gaps in it."

"Something there is that doesn't love a wall," I start to say to him, then do, because he's an English teacher too—on occasion only, now that he's retired.

He picks up on the Frost allusion. "Well, two can't pass abreast through them, but there're gaps just the same, and big."

"And apparently Nature wants the dam down."

"May be, but I don't," he says, "and this is my slice of river here, my stones, my time and energy, and I'm going to put it back up. Guidry's shamed me. A man can take what Nature deals him, until some man shames him into resisting, and repairing."

"Or some woman," I say. "They're much better at shaming you into doing things than men are."

I want to remind him of Emerson's "Hamatreya," a poem in which Earth mocks boastful men who claim ownership of the soil, but I let it go. Besides, this is river and stones, and maybe they're different, though I don't see how: Seems to me a river's even more unclaimable than dirt, since it moves away always. Maybe the stones. Maybe you can claim them, since they stay pretty much where you put them until a great surge from high in the hills rolls them around. Whatever. Philosophy's wearisome out here, with so many things to look at and so many things to do. The water's as clear as newly Windexed glass, polished almost, and slick except where it ripples thin across the stony bottom.

"When it's like this and that's most of the time," Winship is saying as we look out across the wide, flat bed, made that way years ago when he brought in a dragline and reworked the channel, "you've got twenty-six gallons a second going under the bridge, maybe thirty."

Doesn't sound like much, I'm thinking, but then I remember how short a second is and how much twenty-six gallons of water weighs, well over a hundred pounds, and I am impressed. When you try to hold it back, you're even more impressed.

"When they were setting the pilings on the highway overpass downstream back in the fifties, they asked my grandfather to help them out by pumping all he could onto the fields, which he did, and he slowed this stream to a trickle. That was a lot of water to dump, but he did it, with that old one-cylinder engine pounding away and the eight-inch take-up pipe humming. It helped, they told him later, and they thanked him."

"And it all came back to the river," I muse. "Went down to bedrock, which isn't far, and came right back to the river."

"He slowed it down, don't you see, which is all they wanted."

But back to the dam. It's only when you try to tell twenty-six gallons of water a second that the trip it's making is interfering with something you want to do that you get a notion exactly what you're dealing with. You can build and build the dam, but ultimately twenty-six gallons of that water is going to go on downriver every second, come hell or—you know. You may make it pause and reflect, but it will go on down, sure as sin in the inner city.

So I say to Winship, "Do you want to get down there and start repairing it now, or do you want to go have another beer and think about it some more."

"Well, it's late," he says, "so we'll do it tomorrow, when we're fresh—early, before beer call. I want to be able to float Guidry's hat by dark. I want him to have to *swim* to check his lines."

So it is agreed: Tomorrow we'll rebuild the dam.

Early the next morning, while Bob is off in town running errands, my son and I slip down to the river and start on the dam, almost finishing repairs before Bob shows up. He pitches in then and flings shovels of sand and silt against the upwater wall, so that the current carries the finer aggregate in among the rocks and seals the dam tighter.

Even at that, water spouts all along the interior perimeter. But before the sun is mid-morning high the level of the water has risen until it slips around the edge of our barrier and begins to spill across the top.

"Guidry might not float his hat," Bob says, "but he'll find perilous footing toward the other bank. Hard work makes a dam after all, huh?"

"Yeah," I say, "but you still have twenty-six gallons a second going off to the Colorado."

"True, but as Mr. Pate would say, we *slown*

it down some. Everything goes off to somewhere. We could use Frost again here, Ruffin. 'West-Running Brook'—we've made this river stand still and dance, but still it runs away. As Frost puts it, 'It seriously, sadly, runs away.'"

I am studying the boy balancing his way along the stones of the dam, his arms out wide in the mounting sun like something about to take flight. "'The stream of everything,' Frost says. 'And it is time, strength, tone, light, life, and love . . . .'"

The boy has reached the other side and turned around. He comes back toward us, feeling out with his bare feet one slick stone at a time, his eyes fixed straight ahead, while the water sings and gurgles beneath him, off to the north, off to wherever it is going.

Travels with Germann, in Search of Exotics

It is late October, still early and plenty dark, but in the starlight I can make out wheel ruts of the road that skirts what in the spring were oat patches, now little more than fields of mesquite, with clumps here and there taller than a man. Virulent stuff, mesquite will absorb a lightly traveled caliche road in a season.

I am on the Winship ranch easing along before the sun, looking for exotics: deer, not dancers. My companion and guide is a six-month-old dachshund named Germann (hard *G* as in *girdle*) who as Resident Dog at the ranch simply assumed an invitation. He's ahead of me on the road, zipping back and forth, nose to the ground, but he comes back from time to time to check in, report his findings.

I'm carrying a '94 Winchester, not so much for deer as for protection against Indians who might still roam these parts. The cavalry was supposed to have rounded them up over a hundred years ago, but you never know when they might have missed one, and West Texas Indians—Lippan Apache or Kiowa or Comanche—are sudden and vicious. Mississippi Indians are inclined to trade their way out of crisis, discuss issues first—powwow, you know—and, when pushed, they are much more likely to just walk off or throw rocks at you. These Indians out here will leave your hide stretched in the sun. Germann's finely tuned to snoop them out. I watch his dark shape zip across the path right, then left.

As I approach one of the corn feeders, which whirred a few minutes ago, I see flashes of white in the dark. They are of no more interest to me than Germann was to them. I haven't shot at a white-tail in thirty years. You can smother it with onions and sauces or grind it up with a double helping of pork, and white-tail still tastes like what it is. Not so Sika or Axis. But this is not about the taste of deer.

A whole congregation of shapes crosses the field to my left, a herd of cows that Germann has stirred into motion. Now there's acceptable meat, but it's better to bring it home in cellophane with a supermarket bar code and some sort of government stamp that suggests its relative tenderness when properly cooked. Besides, folks ask questions when you string up someone's steer and dress him out without asking first.

Do I stand any chance of killing a deer? Hardly, armed as I am with an old '94 with iron sights and with Germann scouting out there fifty yards raising hell with every shadow. Besides, I've lost my urgency to kill. I'm just not seriously into hunting anymore.

Why do I do it, then? Why do I cross the fields and hills like a hunter when I no longer am? Because I like this land, its smell and look and feel. In the shimmering heat of summer or the bone-deep cold of January, I love walking over it, through the rough mesquite and cedar, up the rocky trails. I like the sound of curly mesquite underfoot, the fragrance of agerita blossoms, and I delight in studying the little ant highways that connect their great circular cities. I love standing high on the bluffs over the oat fields watching night spill out of the valley and fill back up to the brim at day's end. I am mesmerized by the swift, sure-footed deer and keen-eyed turkeys who can detect an eye-blink at fifty yards. I marvel at how clear and cold the water in the river is, how it takes your breath away even in dead summer.

My father-in-law, who's out here with me, killed a big elk in Colorado a couple of weeks ago, and he had to ride back home in a truck with friends while over two hundred pounds of meat, processed by a butcher up there, will fly to Mississippi on a jet in a few days. Now, I might pay the tab to fly home 200 pounds of Australian lobster tails or Alaskan salmon, but not elk. (Remember what I said about white-tail meat? It takes more than onions and sauce to kill elk too.) But my father-in-law likes the taste of elk. He's a serious hunter, and he has the pictures to prove it. If I laid in a pile all the birds and squirrels and deer I've killed in my life and then sat on top of the pile, I doubt the whole heap would amount to a thousand pounds. That would be a spread for the magazines.

I climb into a deer stand to jot down some notes while Germann stands guard. Everywhere I go I take notes. I don't want to forget anything.

The sun's nudging the hills now. A man with leisure might sit and watch night empty out of the valley like a dark liquid draining off until on up late in the morning he can see the bottom of the pan. I'm eternally fascinated by the way this works.

Germann gets antsy after a while. He runs out a few feet from the stand, looks back at me, then moves out a few feet farther. It's as much his show as mine, so I put away my notes and clamber down and follow him. Before I reach the road, he's out of sight.

Drawn by his booger bark at the end of the field, I round a clutter of boulders and find him squared away before a bull who's decided not to be bullied by a dog not much larger than a rat. Head down, horns poised, he's ready to take on his bouncing, hackled attacker. When I step out in the open, Germann looks back at me, then toward the bull. He charges, turns sideways, rips off a string of yaps. It's in High German, but I still remember enough to translate roughly: "OK, big boy, this guy with the rifle behind me here's my buddy and he's hell on bulls. Hates bulls worse'n he does modern rhetoricians. If you don't want to get a dose of lead up the nose, you better head your butt on back to that herd."

It's powerful language for one so young. The bull snorts once and turns and lopes away. Germann calms down, satisfied. A good soldier, he knows that in a confrontation it's not your size that counts—it's the artillery and cavalry behind you. Germann's no more in the mood to kill than I am, but I suspect he'd hang a tooth in that bull in a heartbeat if I encouraged him.

We reach the old wire fence that marks the property line and turn around to start back. The two of us sit on a boulder and loaf a bit first. Time out for ear-rubbing, some R & R.

We'll go back empty-handed, Germann and I, home to one of Shirley's famous breakfast casseroles. This afternoon we'll take to the hills.

Would I shoot an exotic if I saw one? If Germann permitted an Axis with thirty-four-inch horns to come within a stone's throw of me and I had time to get the '94's sights trained on him, I might. But again, probably not. This is not about killing.

Keeping Hog Vigil in Segovia

"So . . . ." Winship draws the word out a long time, then shakes his big intelligent head, now thoroughly grayed over, though his eyes sparkle with the same life and depth of knowledge they must have had almost from the beginning. "So, I think that you ought to take a gun."

We're sitting on the porch of the old wing of the ranch house, where I've sat with him year in and year out for well over a decade, discussing plans for tomorrow. My son is along, as he almost always is these days, since Bob's ranch is one of Matt's favorite places to be. In fact, he may know much of the lay of the land better than I do. When he goes exploring, he is not apt to be put off by the kinds of impediments that might encourage a man considerably along in years and tonnage to seek a path of less resistance. When he goes, he goes the way a thirteen-year-old boy is likely always to go: full speed ahead, damn the mesquites and cedars and limestone cliffs. And the hogs. As we sit talking, the boy's somewhere down on the river. I think. I hope.

Winship has just given me a run-down on the hog situation, as he calls it, a peril that has deepened in seriousness over the past few years and has recently become a major menace. To hammer home my appreciation of the gravity of the problem, he recalled a couple of recent confrontations with Russian Boars, one in which a man got between a sow—when one refers to Russian Boars, he makes no distinction between male and female, since either can carve you up like a pumpkin—and her piglets and lost a good portion of his life for his folly, another in which Bob's very own son had a big hog lope along beside his truck on the top of Hill Three, daring him to stop and get out and scrimmage. Unarmed, the younger Winship did not take him up, though he was a star once upon a time for the SHSU football team—the son, not the hog.

Then Bob pointed out again the big black, heavily tusked boar hanging above the fireplace in the room behind us, looking for all the world as if he took a running start, leapt, and drove his satanic head through concrete blocks on the outside and stone on the inside and simply stuck there, glaring and daring, ready to slash anything within reach. A four-hundred pounder, Bob emphasized, though I remember the tonnage from the first time he announced it, three years ago. The head hangs above the bleached skull of a forty-pound catfish that another of his sons caught on a trotline in the river. There's a neat little hole in the center where the .22 tamed the fish for the trip home. Things grow big out here and require considerable management to be subdued to the useful and the good.

I rare back in my chair and sip from my glass of Ste. Genevieve Texas Red, 1998. "If them pigs is that big of a threat," I say, using the vernacular, which seems less trouble in the valley than being proper, "then I'll tote artillery tomorrow."

"Take my .240," he offers.

"Too much trouble to lug back in there where that boy's going to drag me. I've got a couple of .45's with me—thought I'd target practice some.

I'll strap on the Desert Eagle, which I need to start breaking in anyway." I am proper again.

"That the big one that Clint Eastwood used in . . ."

"Smaller. Called the Uzi Eagle or Baby Eagle. It's a .45"

"A .45 would flatten on their skulls, bounce right off."

"I have a lot of confidence in 230-grain Hydrashocks," I tell him. "Lots of energy. It would probably go through as smoothly as that .22 did through the catfish skull."

"It's like shooting a Cape Buffalo," he says. "If one comes at you, he'll be coming head-on, with one hell of a helmet of bone protecting what little brain he has. A neck or chest shot's out, because that hide along there is two inches thick—ask anybody who's had to dress one of those things. Ask me. You've read Hemingway. Remember what he said about the Cape Buffalo?"

"Yeah, but unless you've imported something I don't know anything about, we won't run across a Cape Buffalo or Black Rhino back in there."

"The skull on a Russian Boar is just about as thick . . ."

"I was thinking more of an eye shot. By the time that Hydrashock gets through churning around in his brain vault, everything in there will be liquid."

He grins big. Snorts. Sips his wine. "Eye shot, my aspidistra. With a hog coming on at full steam, tossing his tusks around like a Gypsy wheeling knives, you couldn't hit an eye with a shotgun."

"Well," I say, "I don't mean to challenge your authority here, but I'm carrying a .45 and hoping for the best. I ask for your blessing."

He gives it.

So it is that up in the morning the next day

Matt and I are making our way along what is called the Spring Draw by all who know it, a deep, forked ravine that runoff from the plateau above has cut out of pure limestone over millennia. For some reason, every time we come out, he has to go exploring back in here, as if something might have changed, as if some great hand has shifted the rock faces or moved the giant elm he always has to see.

This is a virtual wilderness cathedral we're in, with stone walls rising upwards of a hundred feet on each side. Cedars and scrub oak spring out of every little cleavage that holds enough dirt for rooting, and where the soil has gathered in deep pockets elms grow tall, sometimes almost to the level of the rim.

Even with the sun directly overhead, the light down in here is muted, dreamlike and eerie, like we're in another world, and it's probably twenty degrees cooler than the mesquite flats we've just come from.

Along the little creek that runs down the middle of the draw, dribbling water in even the driest of seasons, the ground is pulverized by thousands of hoofprints, like a holding pen for cattle, only what has made these sharp little indentations are deer and aoudad sheep and . . . and hogs. There are places where you'd swear someone has run a breaking plow, so deep and wide are the gouges made by hogs rooting for grubs, or whatever they think is worth eating down under the leaves. I keep my hand on the Eagle as we advance up the draw, heading for higher ground and rougher places, where the going at times will require us to drop onto all fours and scramble along like the hooved and hairy creatures that roam up in here. I make the boy stay close, just in case.

But today there is only peace in this kingdom of the beasts. Wherever the hogs are that plowed this ground, they apparently have little interest in our little intrustion. For this I am glad—I don't want to test the .45 in combat. The boy seems not at all worried, for what he knows of hogs is bacon and ham and sausage. But for one flash of a brown creature with horns, we have seen no other living creatures. Once I heard what might have been a grunt, but when I turned, hand on the Eagle, nothing moved.

He plays around near the giant elm that he has come so much to love and climbs up and down the limestone cliffs. After a while he comes back to where I am seated on a log and asks if I might shoot the pistol. What a question.

He sits down beside me on the log, and I slowly take down a two-inch-thick cedar five yards out, one .45 round at a time. Somewhere toward the end of the second clip, it teeters and topples. I don't know whether he is impressed so much by my marksmanship as by my persistence. I have three loaded clips in reserve, just in case. The main thing is that there's not a chance under the sun that any game, including hogs, is within a mile of that draw by now. It ain't how good a shot you are, after all, but how much noise you can make.

By the time he's ready to go, we are scratched and filthy and bruised from clambering over rocks and slashing through thick cedar, and I am drenched with sweat. The boy walks ahead, jaunty, still brimming with energy, while I bring up the rear, bearing the artillery, weary but still on hog vigil, as I will be until we clear the mesquites and see the house.

"So the hogs didn't eat you," Winship says as I approach the screened-in porch—Matt's gone on off down to the river, bundle of energy that he is.

"Nope. They're saving us for another day. Let's toast my survival. See can you find me a beer, Bobby Lee."

Fishing Among the Stars

The western sky having fallen to full dark, it's well into the night now and I am walking along a field road at the Winship ranch, going fishing with my son, age ten, who's facing a homework-free weekend. He is taking the absence of homework well, I think. He has not complained about it a single time.

Tomorrow we'll be scouting for leaves, though, to complete his science project. While I am off in San Antonio at a conference, Uncle Bob, as he calls Winship, will roam the hills with him in search of leaves we cannot find in East Texas. It is all the schoolwork he is willing to bear on a trip to the ranch.

But tonight we are fishing. And what we are fishing for cannot be found in the crystal clear river that cuts across the corner of Bob's place. Or maybe they can.

See, we are fishing for satellites. Out here there is little competition from the glow of civilization—stars stand out so bright and sharp that they almost hurt the eyes. The glare of Segovia Truck Stop, a few miles off, is only a minor nuisance.

We assume our spot high in the rocks at the foot of Hill Three, the northernmost hill that stretches back from the river valley like a stubby finger. Germann, Bob and Shirley's dachshund, is with us, and he is standing guard against all evil, two-footed or four or none or more. He checks in with us every few minutes to let us know that all is safe on the northern front. We are armed with only my Leatherman tool, which puts us at poor disadvantage should Kiowas or Comanches spill down out of the hills. It has all the appearance of a peaceful night.

To fish for satellites, you need only patience and a set of eyes, which you cast here and there in the broad expanse of Texas sky, drag slowly across, reel in, and cast again, and you do this until against that great speckled dome you see something moving, a simple point of light that zigzags a little, like it's weaving its way among the stars, dodging them. You must be certain it has no green light or red light attached to it, a sure sign it's a plane. This is the way it is done.

You see how many you can spot in an hour, maybe make it a game with your companion, or with yourself. It's a fine form of fishing, since you don't have to lug cumbersome tackle or haul a heavy stringer back or get all messy cleaning what you've caught. Sometimes out here I will lie back in the bed of my pickup and have a couple of beers while I'm fishing. (Of course I have to sit up to take sips of beer—anyone who tells you you can drink beer lying down is simply lying another way.) I've done the same thing on a boat off the Mississippi Coast, but the lights of Biloxi and Pascagoula interfere. Out here, though, out here . . . .

I want to tell the boy that when you spot a satellite, you are seeing the sun reflected, like the moon—the sun is still shining over the curve of the earth and deep into space and the little things we send up there throw back its light. But I know from decades of dealing with literature that to over-analyze is to risk the loss of magic, so I keep my mouth shut and wait for him to ask if there's something he wants to know about what we're seeing. He says nothing.

Then he gets the munchies—fishing always make you hungry, you know—so I rummage around in my vest and find a box of Altoids and a bag of cinnamon jellybeans one of my graduate students gave me. He votes jellybeans, so we split them. Germann politely turns down both. He's probably thinking as he heads out to scout again, *Always candy and breath mints and stuff. Don't nobody tote bones anymore. Don't nobody think about the dog.*

As I lie back on a boulder and cast across the sky, I get to thinking about how down at the river we could study the stars on the surface of the big still pool behind a sandbar and maybe spot a satellite scooting through the water, but I don't mention it because Matt would want to go down there and try it, and it's already late and the river is all the way at the other end of the property. So I keep quiet and fish on into the night, while he lies beside me doing the same. Lord knows what he's thinking. But I hope it's good, and I hope he'll remember this night sometime far off in the future when maybe he takes his own son out under a wide Texas sky to fish among the stars.

In Search of a Tumbler

It's late November and Matt and I are at the Winship ranch, standing in the middle of a field road while the sun crawls up over one of the hills behind us. I'm on my knees searching for insect activity around an old cow pie, but nothing's moving. The boy's looking down at me the way a person looks toward the sun, one eye closed a little tighter than the other, but he's facing away from the sun, so the squint is simple incredulity.

"They do *what*?"

"They take the shi . . . they take a clump of dung, or manure, and form a ball, and they roll it—"

"That's one of the grossest things you've ever told me," he says, "and maybe I don't want to hear any more."

"That's up to you."

He leans closer to me. "You mean there's a bug that takes cow poop—" See, an eleven-year-old boy can't stand this kind of thing: it bugs him, as it were. He's got to push it, even if it is unsavory.

"Or horse, rhino, whatever's handy. But it's got to be fresh, and since Uncle Bob has moved the cows off the place, we're not likely to find—"

"There's deer poop."

"Yeah, but that's already in pellets, sort of like balls, and it'd be cheating for them—"

"So he rolls this stuff up into a ball, the way you would a snowball, and takes it home with him?"

"Yes," I say, "that's precisely what he does. Sometimes a couple will do it together, the male guiding the ball in front while the female pushes from behind. They'll actually tumble over the ball, which is why they're called tumble bugs."

"I can understand why insects and animals do lots of things, but I can not—I do *not* understand why anything would fool with that stuff. I mean, what do they do with the ball when they get it home? Do their kids play with it, or what?"

I laugh at that. Who wouldn't? The image of a bunch of tumble bug babies scooting a ball of dung around is—well, it's an unusual picture.

I try to explain it to him. "They feed off the ball of dung, then the female lays her eggs in it, and the offspring eat from the inside when they hatch."

"If you're trying to make me feel any better about it, it's not working. They *eat* that stuff?"

"It's what people in sophisticated circles call an *acquired taste*. Look here. To them it's a lot less offensive than, say, gummy bears. As a matter of fact, tumble bug children would probably be grossed out by much of the stuff y'all eat."

"Give me gummy bears any day," he says.

"At least what they eat is digestible. Gummy bears are not."

"I don't know what you have against gummy bears, but you never have anything good to say about them."

"Right. Mainly because there's only one good thing *to* say about them—they are cheap. You guys can chew a handful all day and never get them down. They're the closest thing to a perpetual snack that I know about."

"I'm glad you never brought anything like that home. You know, a ball of—"

"I wouldn't," I say. "We all have to deal with it at the office from time to time, but we try not to bring it home."

We drop the matter at that and start searching the fields and mesquites for butterflies. It's obviously not a tumble bug day. My daughter, four years older than Matt, is a few insects shy of the sixty she wants to assemble for a project due in biology, a tumble bug among them.

Some of the butterflies that work across the fields and at the edge of the mesquite are unusual in color, quite spectacular, so we try to catch as many different kinds as we can. Along one of the roads leading through a mesquite thicket to the hills we spot a little clump of blooming desert bushes I cannot identify, and they are aflame with Sleepy Oranges, Dog Faces, Common Sulphurs, Gorgone Checkerspots, and Juba Skippers—names we do not know now but will learn with the help of books borrowed from Dr. Jimmie Long of the SHSU Biology Department. Before long we have ziplock bags fluttering with little wedges of color that look like pieces of a jigsaw puzzle we might have popped from the landscape or the sun.

Later, back at the house, we assign them to the cold dark winter of the freezer, where they will not flutter long.

As we wrap things up, he says, "The only thing worse would be a buzzard." He's still on the tumble bug business.

"Well, Nature has a purpose for both. Part of the recycling process. If it weren't for buzzards, there'd be dead things lying all over, smelling the place up. On the other hand, I'll bet you there's no provision at all in Nature for human children to eat gummy bears. As a matter of fact, it's downright unnatural for you to eat rubber. Your digestive system wasn't designed for it."

"You ought to lighten up on gummy bears."

"And you ought to let the tumble bugs and buzzards alone. Deal?"

"Deal," he says.

Later that evening when I walk into the bedroom to undress for a shower, something on my pillow catches my eye. I lean and look closely. It is a tumble bug, about an inch long, and he's just sitting there, like he's waiting for me to go get a ziplock from my vest, which I do. In short order he too is experiencing the coldest, darkest winter of his life.

"Uncle Bob or PawPaw must have put him there," I tell my son, who's marveling at this miracle.

"We didn't tell them we were looking for a tumble bug, did we?"

I shake my head. "No. I didn't. Did you?"

"No." He hesitates a few seconds, then adds, "I wonder what it means."

"What *what* means?"

"What it means when you find a tumble bug laying your pillow. I would wonder about it if I found one on mine. Kind of like you would if a buzzard kept circling you."

"It doesn't mean anything," I say. "I'm just glad it happened."

"That's almost like Tooth Fairy stuff," he says, as we lean on the old split-rail fence in front of the house watching the last light fade over the hills. Soon it will be time to watch for satellites. "Maybe there's a Tumble Bug Fairy."

"May be," I say, my eyes fixed on a point of light moving from the east, "may be."

Philosophy and Science at Breakfast

Scene set: I walk into the Segovia Truck Stop diner and at a corner table join Winship and an electrical engineer buddy of his up from Houston, a guy named Dan. They are in a deep discussion. Part of this is made up, but I can't say for sure which—it was early, before I had had a full cup of coffee. You just can't remember every word that's said when stuff like this happens. You fill in the gaps with what you think was said. I know: I could lie and say it's all true, and you wouldn't know any better. But I won't.

"Take the breakfast we have coming, these Western omelettes," Winship is saying, looking wise. "It's a grand concoction of eggs, cheese, peppers, and ham. A chicken will be involved in it, several of them, but a pig will be *committed* to it. Big-time."

Dan sips his coffee and sets it down. "I'll bet nobody asked the pig. Doesn't commitment require conscious consideration of options? Given a choice, would the pig have elected to participate in our breakfast?"

Winship wags his head. "As an eater, perhaps, not as the eaten. Then one might just as well ask whether the chicken was consulted."

"But the chicken has little to lose," Dan says. "The pig loses everything."

I break in: "Nobody knows how a chicken feels about having her eggs taken away." Then: "We could be getting into a gender-discrimination issue here as well. Consider this—only female chickens lose at breakfast. For lunch and dinner it's probably equal opportunity, except for Thanksgiving and Christmas, when I understand that hens, which usually have more fat on them, are more desirable for the table. At breakfast, though—"

"Well," says Dan, "the gender issue fades if you regard each egg as a potential chicken—you could argue that at least nine chickens, of undetermined gender, will perish to feed us this morning. There will have to be three eggs in each of those omelettes."

Winship has a glint in his eye. "In this case we know which came first, the chicken, not the egg. First the chicken, otherwise no egg." He's enjoying this.

So am I: "That may be. But I wonder whether either of you can tell me which came first, the chicken or the pig?"

They stare at me for what seems like a full minute.

"Are we dealing with ontology here?" Winship asks.

Dan chimes in. "Maybe *oncology*, if either one of them had a tumor. Or *oinkology*, if we ventured into pig language. Or *arkology*, if we're considering which came off the ark first."

But Winship seriously pursues: "Well, I think we've ventured outside the parameters of ordinary philosophical debate here, but in the case of the omelette, the chicken came first, since the ham is inside the egg part of the omelette, not lying on top of or beside it."

"What's the term for the egg part of the omelette?" Dan asks. "Is it called a blanket, a wrap, what?"

Winship and I shrug, and I motion a waitress over. She sidles up. "What do you call the egg part of an omelette?"

Unsmiling, she works on a big wad a gum a few seconds, then stares out toward the cliff across the interstate. "We call it the *egg part.*"

She is satisfied, we are satisfied, so she goes on about her business.

I persist: "My question was, which came first, the chicken or the pig? It's not the chicken the cook's putting the ham inside. It's the egg part. So all you've proven is that the egg came before the pig."

"Without the chicken, you wouldn't have the egg," Dan points out.

Winship grins big and slaps his hands together. "Well, we're back to where we started."

I sip my coffee and go again: "We have to get a focus on this thing. Are we limiting ourselves to the matter of the omelette or the egg, chicken, and pig before they came together *in* the omelette?"

"There *is* no chicken *in* it," Winship says. "And what is this *we* business? You're the one who brought up the chicken/pig issue. You are—"

"Bob, if you consider an egg—"

Dan clears his throat. "You know, I have been an engineer for over four decades, and I never did see any real sense in arguing over things like the chicken and the egg. We have both, and we are glad for both, and there's nothing to be gained by trying to determine which came first because there is no answer to the question. Now, take the tree-falling-in-the-forest problem, which is equally perplexing to most people. Because here you're dealing not with philosophy but with science, there is an answer, a logical one."

Winship snorts. "OK, then, Dan, if a tree falls in the forest and there's no one to hear it, does it make a sound?"

"No. It creates waves that can be translated into audible sound by an instrument like the human ear. But it does not create what we refer to as sound. All sound is merely vibration anyway. The ear translates vibration into what we refer to as sound."

"I buy that," Winship says.

I interrrupt: "Why can't philosophy and science be more compatible bedfellows?"

"What do you mean?" Winship is staring at me.

"Well, I started off in engineering, I switched to English. I'm interested in the tree falling in the forest but also in the chicken and the egg."

"Must be the Renaissance mind at work," Winship says. "A balance of the right and left sides of the brain, you know. The guy's helping wire my house, but he talks about literature while he's doing it."

"I always figured he just wasn't focused, Bob." Dan has squared around in his chair to look at me. "So where are you going with this? How do you fuse the chicken/egg problem with the tree falling in the forest?"

"Well," I say wisely, "how long would you say we've been waiting for our omelettes?"

Winship shrugs. "Maybe ten minutes." He holds an MA in English. He is not always precise.

Dan looks at his watch. "Exactly twelve." Remember, he's an engineer.

"OK: You have a chicken and a pig in the forest, standing right beside a big tree. The tree falls. Do the chicken and the pig hear the tree fall?"

"Of course they do," Dan says. Winship nods vigorously.

I give them my sagest look. "No, they do not, because the tree fell on both of them, which explains why our breakfast is so slow coming."

Then the steaming omelettes are before us on

the table, and quiet descends as science and philosophy yield to the simple pleasure of three men having breakfast.

Lot Lizards in the Desert

I'm in the Segovia Truck Stop diner with Mr. Pate and Winship, and I can't see that their conversation is going anywhere in particular, so I change the subject. "Do you guys know what a lot lizard is?"

Mr. Pate shakes his head and Winship grunts, squints his eyes at me. "Can't say that I do. I figure it's not an ingredient in a Western omelette."

"Right," I say, then tell them what I know about lot lizards, a term used for prostitutes who work the truck stops and rest stops. I once had a creative writing student—husband was a trucker—who used the term in a story, and when I asked her about it, she filled me in on this particular tangent of the profession. (Said her husband never experienced one first-hand but that he saw them in the lots a lot.)

"Hmmm," Winship says, cocking his head wisely to the side the way he often does, "bet I've seen 'm before but didn't know it."

"Well, they don't exactly wear a sign."

"Some might." Mr. Pate is looking across the aisle at a large blond woman hunkered over, working on a world-class stack of pancakes oozing butter at every seam. She fills the better part of her half of the booth. "Look on her shirt."

Winship squints and looks. "I'll be damned."

"What?" I can't see anything unusual about her.

"Look on her—just above her—"

Winship helps him out, very quietly: "Her right breast."

"No, no, Bob, it's her left."

"No, Mr. Pate, it's—"

"Would y'all just stop it? Quit staring at her. I'll check both of them out."

I get up and walk slowly past her, turning my eyes to the hurt point in their sockets, then wheel around at the counter like I've remembered something and come back to the table.

"So what the hell are y'all talking about?"

Mr. Pate leans in toward me. "That's a little green lizard above her left breast."

"Right one," Winship corrects, whispering. "It's *your* right."

The old man gives him a quick look. "Neither *one* of them is mine."

"Perspective is everything, Mr. Pate. You can point to the one on the right and say that's her right one; you ask her to point to her right one, and she'll point to the one you're figuring is her left."

"Yeah, well, I ain't astin' her *anythang.*"

"Would y'all just forget about which one it's above? That is an *alligator.* She's got on an old Izod shirt. It's an alligator, not a lizard."

"May be," Mr. Pate says, "but I sure wouldn't wear one in here."

"You'd be safe if you did," Bob tells him.

"Boy, she fills that thing out." The old man is peeping over the rim of his cup.

"You guys." This whole scene makes me uneasy. She looks like the kind of woman who just might pull a grenade out of her purse, unpin it, and pitch it into your grits.

"Sizable perch that ol' boy's on."

"Mr. Pate!"

Bob confirms: "Yeah, he could roll over three or four times and not fall off."

"Got room for a little house maybe, driveway, swingset for the kids in back—"

I stare into my coffee. "This is the last time I try to do research with you y'all along."

Mr. Pate kicks me under the table and rolls his eyes toward the woman. She's picked up a phone, which they have in each of the booths, and dialed a number. "She's makin' contact."

"Not really a bad-looking woman," Winship observes quietly, "in the face, I mean."

"Man, put on your glasses," I tell him.

"Not saying I'm attracted to her, Ruffin. Just not a bad-looking face."

"Well, hell, Bob, that UPS tractor/trailer idling out there out there's not bad looking, but I wouldn't want to kiss it or dance with it or—."

"There she goes," the old man breaks in. "Off on a call."

The woman has plopped a couple of bucks down on the table, wedged herself out, and shuffled up to the counter to pay her bill. Her pants are incredibly tight, like sausage skins and about that color, and you know that if one little stitch gives way anywhere on the outfit there'll be a sound like thunder and the whole place will come down on us. She makes it out the door.

"Watch her now," Bob says. "See what guy she goes up to."

I stare at the bare table. "What I want to see is a Western omelette in front of me."

Mr. Pate whispers, "There she goes."

The woman lumbers toward a great black diesel tractor, hauls herself up by the handle of the driver's door, unlocks the truck, and squirms into the seat. She wallows around until apparently she is comfortable.

"Lord, she's got a key to his truck," Winship says. "Acts like she lives there."

She leans down and does something, straightens up, and slides on some sunshades. Then the truck comes to life, *vrooom*, *clatter*, *clatter*. The blond adjusts her sunshades, looks over her shoulder, and moves out onto the service road. Soon the big trailer she's pulling rolls down the ramp to the interstate and the truck gets smaller and smaller as it nudges into the pass to the east.

"You see the name on that door?" Winship asks us.

"Part of it," Mr. Pate answers. "*Big Bad* somethin' or other, started with a *M*."

"I hope you guys feel as sheepish as you ought to," I say.

Winship smiles and reaches for his coffee. "What can I say? Maybe were wrong."

I stand up with my notebook and lean forward on the table. "Tell you what, fellas. It's obvious they're having to go out and kill a hog for our breakfast. While we're waiting, I'm going to go check out the bathrooms for graffiti. I'll be back in a few minutes. Y'all try to behave yourselves."

They nod.

"And, Bob."

"Yeah?"

"When the waitress finally does get here with our food, have her bring me bacon instead of sausage."

He nods, grins big.

The Bowhunter Asks for My Bladder

It was early January a few years ago on the Rockpile Ranch, just hours before whitetail season expired, and on a scaffold beside one of the hunters' cabins I had hanging a medium-size Sika buck I'd brought down with my rifle that morning. On the scaffold beside my Sika was a whitetail doe being skinned by a bowhunter.

I had just entered the serious phase of dressing the still-steaming carcass (they call it dressing, when what you're really doing is *undressing*), stripping out all the organs he wouldn't need anymore, when my bowhunter neighbor leaned over with his knife pointed across my shoulder at the Sika's entrails. I was a little uneasy.

"What you gon' do with that bladder?"

I stopped hacking. Hell, I didn't know. Hadn't thought about it. What *can* you do with a deer bladder? You can't eat it, can you? (I don't know that the most exotic restaurant in the world serves deer bladder. Imagine yourself saying to some prissy waiter poised with a delicate gold pen, "Hey, me'n the little lady here've decided on your Big Buck Bladder Platter, baked potato with cheese and chives, house dressin' on the salad.") I guess you do the same thing with it that you do with a hog's bladder or a turkey's or a snake's (if they've got one)—you throw it away. Long gone are the days when some great unwritten code required you to keep and put to use every part of a slaughtered animal. (As neighbor Mr. Pate says, "Buzzards got to eat too.") What was I going to do, make a water jug out of it the way the Comanches did out of buffalo bladders? Not a chance, not when I had a stainless-steel Army canteen. And even if I summoned the nerve to put my lips to the bladder and blow it full of air, my kids sure wouldn't play with it. So I just told him: "Nothing."

"Can I have it?" It was the same tone of quiet urgency somebody across the table would use asking for the piece of prime steak you've been eating the less savory meat from around, saving it for last—the way some people do. His knife was steady, keen, blood all the way up on the handle, and still pointing at my bladder.

Could he have it? Whoa, now. When a fellow asks you whether he can have something you're about to throw away, you just naturally grow thoughtful, even if he's got a sharp knife six inches from your throat. You don't want to loosen your grip until you know for sure that you're not making a big mistake. It's the same care you have to take at a garage sale. You drag out of the shop or attic something that you are absolutely certain isn't worth the effort it would take to burn or bury, toss it on the bargain table, price it at a dollar, and somebody snatches it up. Then you hear him say to a friend on the way down the drive, "Do you know what this *is*? I seen one for a hundred bucks in a antique store in Houston one time—woulda bought it for that if I'd a-had the money. And that damned fool . . . ."

The voice trails off—you're too busy scrambling to re-assess everything to hear how he concludes.

But back to the bladder. What if Sika urine were now an ingredient in expensive cologne and worth five hundred simoleons an ounce at some Parisian perfumery, or a South American doctor had discovered that a thimble of it taken daily would shrink hemorrhoids or a swollen prostate, or a sexologist in Europe had developed from it an anti-impotency elixir advertised in *Hustler* and *American Rifleman* and *Popular Mechanics*? What did this guy want with that little bag of waters? So, with it still hanging in the Sika among the other pinks and purples, wiring and plumbing intact, I just up and asked him, "What the hell for?"

"Well," he said, his eyes secretive, "what I do is I tie it off and take it to the field with me, and when I establish my blind . . . ."

They are so bloody serious about this business, the bowhunters. *Establish his blind.* Like you'd establish a new world order or a wartime beachhead or a trust fund for your kids.

"When I establish my blind, you know, I sprinkle the stuff all around it and on my clothes, dab some on my neck."

"You deliberately put deer piss on yourself?"

"Yeah. You know, it kills the human scent, better'n bakin' soda or oranges or any kind of product that Wal-Mart or Academy sells."

I turned back to my carcass again, thinking *so what if it does?* So you make your blind smell like a Sika buck's latrine. What kind of draw is that? Bruce (Bambi's husband or live-in or counter gender, whatever you'd call him) is bopping along and he smells the stuff and thinks, *Hey, I rekkin I'll go over and check this ol' boy out.* Naw. Won't happen. I don't know about you folks, but I tend to shy away from anything that smells like a urinal unless I really need one. Aw, I know about a buck being concerned about some other big boy pissing on the block, but still . . . .

Winter's the mischief in me (and spring, summer, and fall), so I stood back from the Sika and after noting that my right cheek was colder than the left and I was facing south—that meant the wind had to be from the west—I walked a few feet east and relit my cigar, which during the skinning and gutting I'd let go out. I don't smoke them often, but gutting any kind of animal liberates smells you far prefer cigar smoke to.

"Look here," I said. "There's an easier way." I blew smoke into the wind and it tumbled back on me.

He just stood there.

"Can you smell my cigar?"

He held his nose in the air, worked it around some. "Naw."

"No, you cannot," I said. "And if I had slathered on half a cup of cologne—which I would never do because I don't wear the stuff, even to parties—you couldn't smell it. What does that tell you? What fundamental fact of deer hunting are you observing here?"

After a few seconds he said, "I don't know." Then: "I don't smoke cigars. And I sure as hell don't wear cologne when I hunt."

I narrowed my eyes and studied him long and hard, then walked over to my Sika, where I reached in and separated the bladder from the rest of the entrails, cut and tied it off, and handed it to him. "Merry belated Christmas," I said, "enjoy your golden shower."

Sexing an Armadillo

"So you're telling me," Leroy Brown is saying to Buster Butler as the three of us hunker around the remains of a campfire that two hours earlier cooked our jackrabbit stew, "that they don't have the same kind of equipment that we do?"

It is early March, and we're on the back side of a scrubby hill that thrusts up out of the river valley in Segovia, just three men on a camp-out in the wilds. It was my idea to spend nearly two days out here, sleep under the stars, have a supper of beans and BBQ over an open fire, the next morning fry up bacon and eggs and slices of buttered bread for breakfast, complete with grits, heavy with butter and salted and peppered properly, then finish off with stew made from a fresh-killed jackrabbit for lunch. Much more importantly, I wanted to talk to men whose lives are governed by horses and cows and the weather, whose world has not changed much more than the stars in forty years. I have brought myriad questions for them, these aging cowboys, one nearly fifty, one just over, and they have humored me with a few nuggets of value, but it has come down to this absurd level, as is so often my lot.

"It's a fact. Or if it's there, you can't tell it."

"But they are mammals," I point out, not really wishing to get into this discussion but honor-bound to inject fact when I'm among those who don't care much for them (facts, that is).

"Meaning what?" Leroy asks. That question tells you a lot about Leroy, who finished the third grade at the Segovia school, then scrambled up on the horse that he rode in on and never went back.

"Meaning that they are warm-blooded and bear young and provide milk and that the equipment is there."

"I thought mammals had to have hair," Buster says. He lords it over Leroy a lot, since he was within three weeks of finishing the fifth grade when a full-time job lured him to a feedstore in Junction.

Leroy drains the last of his coffee from the stainless steel Texas Department of Corrections coffee cup I gave him and reaches and pours up another. "Armadillers ain't got hair, so they must not be mammals."

"Whales is mammals, but they ain't got hair. Ain't that right, Perfesser?"

I nod. "Lots of mammals don't have hair."

"Mammals, smammals." Leroy shakes a Camel out of a crumpled pack and leans and fetches a stick from the fire and lights up and throws the stick back. "Then how come they ain't got the equipment?"

I look from one to the other. "Guys, they *do* have the equipment. It's just not all that easy to find among the scales."

"You ever seen it?" Leroy asks me.

"No. I've never had a good reason to look. But you can bet Buster's horse that it's there."

"Ain't *nobody* gon' put *my* horse down on a bet about a armadiller, expecially when it comes to trying to figger out whether one is a boy or a girl."

"Well," Leroy says, "I don't want you to think I make a habit of it, but I pried the legs apart on the last one I shot and I didn't see anythang that looked right down there."

Buster snorted. "Aw, man that is some kinda sick."

"Naw, it ain't. It's what is called intellectual curiosity. Inquirin' minds want to know. That kind of thang.

"How you could *really* tell," Leroy goes on, "is if you had one, say tied to a tree with a strang or something, all you'd have to do would be to trot a female armadiller past him and see would he go after her or not. Then you'd know."

I give him a stern look. "Uh, Leroy, if you can't tell the sex of an armadillo, how are you going to know that it's a female you're running past it or that it's a boy armadillo you have tied to the tree?"

"Good point, Perfesser," Buster says, then to Leroy: "And the one you got tied to the tree might be a homosexual, which would make your experiment mute anyhow."

"*Moot*, not *mute*." I just can't let that kind of thing go.

They look at me. "I always heard *mute*, myself," Leroy says. "What the hell does it mean anyhow?"

"Moot . . . ," I try, but Buster breaks in.

Then Leroy looks sage and says, "I always heard *mute* too." Then: "Buster, there ain't any homosexuals in nature."

"Leroy's a expert on homosexuals, Perfesser."

"*I* ain't one, all I know."

"There is too homosexuals in nature," Buster says. "I heard tell that bats is the worst about that in all of the animal kingdom."

"Bats?" Leroy is animated now. "Where in the hell did you hear that at?"

"Somethin' I seen on the TV."

It is time to get this conversation moving in another directions. "Do y'all know what the word *armadillo* means?"

"Means something ugly and nasty and without the proper equipment to me," Leroy says.

"It means *little armored thing*. That's what the early Spanish explorers called them. *Azotchtli* is the Aztec name: means *turtle rabbit*. Y'all should take notes now, since I might give you a quiz later."

Buster grunts and fires up a cigarette. "He's lordin' it over us again, Leroy. It's what we get for campin' out with a college perfesser."

He stares at me. "You know all about armadillers, but can you tell the sex of one?"

"I never tried. There are limits to my intellectual curiosity. But since they've been around fifty million years, I have a pretty good notion that they have what you call the equipment and they know how to use it."

Buster says, "Somethin' else I heard tell is that if you cut them organs off a armadiller, they are still active."

"The armadillos or the organs?" I ask him.

"The organs," he says. "like lizard tails."

Leroy shakes his head. "That's a big bucket of hog crap is whut. Lord, I'll tell what ain't. Them's the ugliest thangs alive. Except for maybe possums. Do you rekkin a boy armadiller really sees anythang a-tall purty in a girl armadiller? I mean, even with a nice little hat and sundress on and make-up, she'd still be scaly and ugly as sin."

"Well," Buster says, "when he comes courtin', I don't imagine that it's the face end he's aimin' at."

"They didn't come north of the Rio Grande until around 1850," I tell them. "As a matter of fact, until the land bridge formed that joined the two continents, they were confined to South America."

Leroy stands and stretches. "Yeah, well, they takin' over the whole country now."

"Can't tolerate cold weather," I explain, "so

they're not likely to spread beyond the South and Southwest."

"Yeah, Buster, the Perfesser knows all about armadillers, but he can't tell us shit about how to tell the sex of one."

"I'll just bet you that I can, if you'll bring me one, preferably dead."

"You are on." Then Leroy brushes his jeans off and tosses the rest of his coffee on the fire. "I'll go see can I get one for you to take a look at." He walks off toward the truck, where his Winchester '94 is. "I'll be back terreckly, with a armadiller, if I'm lucky."

"How come you rekkin so many of'm gets killed in the road?" Buster asks me after Leroy has disappeared into the mesquite.

"Because, for one thing, they are not the fastest horse on the track, in their heads or their feet. In their little pea-sized brains they have somehow developed the notion that their armor will protect them from anything."

"Even Detroit. God, I'd hate to be a armadiller," he says.

"How can you say that? Don't you figure that they would hate to be us? Every animal is content to be what he is, except us. We're the only really screwed-up creature in nature."

"At least it's easy to tell a male human from a female."

"For us, yeah. I imagine armadillos don't have any trouble figuring out which is which either."

"Perfesser, he's gon' put you in a tight spot if he comes back with a armadiller."

"I know that. Do you think he'll get one?"

"Oh yeah. May take him till dark and a half, but you'll hear that 30-30 bark, and he'll come wagging one in for you."

"I was afraid of that."

"You not gon' be able to tell. You know that,

don't you? Gon' be hard to have to admit it. He'll spread the word all over Segovia and Junction that you ain't as smart as people think." He smiles broadly. "Or you can lie, since, dumb as Leroy is, ain't no way he'd know the difference."

"Oh, I'll be able to tell." I am lying big–time, but I can't let him know it.

We put the fire out and split up. I have about three miles to walk through some pretty heavy brush to get back to the Winship place. Buster's on a quarter horse named Earl that has more sense than he does, so he has no worry about getting home. Leroy'll bring our camping gear in the truck to the ranch later. First he's got to check on a couple of fences.

A few minutes after I quit hearing the clop of Buster's horse, I pull out my cell and dial up Gerry Etheredge, veterinarian extraordinaire back in Huntsville. I know he'll know how. He'll just have to know how.

Charlie Swartz Talks about the Big Bang

When I consider the Big Bang, that cosmic party that got out of hand a few eons before Wal-Mart came along, it is not often or with serious intent, rather with a whimsical, casual, so-it-happened-or-it-didn't sideways glance, the way you'd greet the news that someone off in Saudi Arabia had discovered that a certain sand, when consumed daily in a molasses paste, will prevent you from becoming severely mature, or old as dirt. It is knowledge that, even when taken in minor doses, does scarcely more than disconcert, since it would be a hard choice between having to eat a bowl of that sticky sand every day and dying at a reasonable age and not having to eat it.

I occasionally bring such deep subjects up with a friend of mine out in Junction, Charlie Schwartz, who hasn't been troubled with the burden of higher education and can think and speak on his own without the clutter of authoritative citations. Charlie, hired because of his skills and not his education, is retired from high school football coaching and now runs a few head of cows on just over a thousand acres of scrub oak and mesquite, what's left of the family ranch. Much of it is high ground and rough, but a corner of the property dips down into the lush valley of the Johnson Fork, giving him that coveted river footage that he could sell in a heartbeat to some wealthy retiree out of Houston or Dallas, if he could bring himself to do it, which he can't. The third-generation heritor, he is no more likely than the ones before him to make a profit on the place, though his income from big-city deer hunters, coupled with Social Security, gets him and wife Betty by. The cows are there because they always have been. He says that his needs are small anyway. When you look around the house and notice what's parked in the carport, you figure that they probably are.

We're sitting on his porch steps drinking beer late in the day, watching the stars just begin to burn holes through the velvet over us. Charlie's nursing a cigarette, getting every millimeter out of it before the fiberglass smoke fouls up his lungs and makes him cough, and I am taking an occasional draw off a cigar, a tiny pleasure I permit myself out here, where if anyone says something to you about smoking or drinking beer, you just tell him to go shove a cactus up his ass.

"I can't see what difference it makes," he tells me, "this business about the Big Bang. It won't make us feel any better about ourselves, whatever we find out up there, just make us feel littler and littler."

I'm thinking about Copernicus starting all this, but if I bring it up, he'll just snort and say that he never heard of anybody named Copernicus.

"Has to be foreign, with a name like that," he'd say. "And what could his folks be thinking, making him tote a moniker like that the rest of his days?"

"His friends called him Nick," I could say to him, "and he was Polish." But I'd just be wasting breath. He'd conclude with something tacky about the Poles, about how they couldn't hold Hitler up longer than a bunch of Boy Scouts. He's pretty much down on everybody these days—his teeth are giving him trouble.

"You ever wonder how come we always look *up* for the truth?" he asks me.

"Maybe because it's toward Heaven?"

"The people down in Australia look up too, but it's a different direction from where we look. It'd be down for us. We've always got our eyes toward the sky and our mouths open, like turkeys in the rain. Maybe the answer ain't up." He shakes another wrinkled cigarette from its pack, straightens it with his hard fingers, zips a match on the steps, lights up. "Maybe it ain't nowhere."

"But we're hell-bent to try to find it."

"Yeah," he says, "and the way we go about it is awfully expensive. Used to be, faith did the trick, and that was a hell of a lot cheaper, only now we got to have some sort of scientific proof, evidence we can haul into a laboratory, or trap in numbers on a page. You figure we any closer to God up there than we are down here?"

He reaches down and scoops a handful of dirt from the base of some sort of leathery shrub that survives the savage summers out here. "You reckon there's more God in a handful of Martian soil than there is in this?" He lets part of it sift through his fingers onto the concrete step. "Hell naw there's not." He throws the rest back under the bush. "At least we know there's bugs in our dirt."

He continues. "Somebody tells me about the Big Bang and looks smug and says what do you think about that, and what I say is, 'All right, I can picture this little ball of whatever it is no bigger than a pin head hangin' out there in the dark. It's hard, but I can imagine it.' But what I want to say to them is, 'Just where in the hell did that little ball come from and why did it explode? Who lit the damn fuse?'"

I nod and study his face, tightened on itself from the cigarette smoke.

"See, even if we buy the Big Bang theory, we

are no closer to understanding the whences and wherefores and whatifs of it all than we were before. The universe is a grand complexity and the grain of sand is a small complexity, but they are complexities just the same, and very likely neither will ever be fully explained. But we go on trying, making ourselves miserable."

Sometimes I marvel at the way he can express himself, but I don't say so. "Reminds me of a poem by Cummings," I say, "titled '[pity this busy monster manunkind].' He makes reference to man playing 'with the bigness of his littleness,' deifying a razor blade into a mountain range, his instruments doing little to set his mind at ease. Or Frost's 'The Bear,' in which he has the poor, confused human being nervously pacing like an imprisoned bear, with the telescope at one end of his cage and the microscope at the other, and neither of the instruments giving him much peace or hope."

He laughs. "Well, poetry's a bigger mystery to me than the universe."

"By the way," I say, "that Cummings poem has the first use of the terminal *not* that I know about: 'Pity this busy monster manunkind, / *not*.'"

"I'd of thought *Saturday Night Live* come up with it. Shows what I know."

He goes in and gets us another couple of beers. When he comes back out he settles beside me on the step and starts up again. "We been rummaging around finding out things about ourselves for a long time now, and we still get born and we still die, and the seasons go around like they've always done. We look at a baby and we know where we come from, and we look at a cemetery and we know where we're going. So we can sit around wondering, squinting through what they call an intellectual fog, maybe get out there and pursue the truth with some kind of instrument. Or we can say to the Devil with it all and go out and romp with the kids and dog or go in and play with the children's momma, neither of which requires much understanding of universal laws, creates anxiety, or raises taxes."

When I leave him, it is full dark. He's lit another cigarette, whose little red speck I see glow and fade behind me until a clump of mesquites slides between us. Stars are firing up in the northern and eastern sky, the way they do, the way they always have, like pinholes in velvet, with no way for us to get to the light on the other side, and no really good reason to want to.

When the Handyman Became a Slave

Sometimes when I'm out here and bored—which is pretty seldom—I drive over to Junction and visit a handyman named Herbert, who will take on just about any job that comes his way. What I know about carpentry, plumbing, mechanic, and electrical work I learned back in Mississippi alongside just such a man. If he's doing something interesting, sometimes I'll pitch in and help out.

Now, Herbert is about five-four and probably weighs just over a hundred pounds, but every ounce of him is muscle and gristle and bone, with prominent veins all up and down his arms. He has very black hair, which never looks like it has had a comb dragged through it, and what people call a hatchet face. I have never had the opportunity to count his teeth, but once I saw where he had taken a bite out of an apple, and I can guarantee you that, judging by that jagged crater, he doesn't have many. He looks like he has been turned over a fire for decades–I guess his constant smoking has done that to him.

For nearly a decade Herbert served as an undertaker's assistant, so some of his most memorable stories came from that period of his life. He loves to tell them while I'm eating a can of Spam or Vienna sausages with crackers. They are far too gruesome to repeat, unless you'd like to learn about how they manage to get arms and legs and other things to behave and how they get gas out of a body that's bloated. I could embalm somebody in the dark.

And if you think an undertaker's assistant is beyond prying open a corpse's mouth and pulling off gold crowns with needle-nose pliers, you'd better back up a couple of spaces and think again. When I asked him how he got away with that, he asked me, "Yevver seen a corpse smile? Nope. They always dead serious. Ain't seen a loved one yet reach over and peel back Uncle Leo's lips to see if them gold crowns is still in there."

As far as that goes, you can't always trust the family. He pried open one guy's mouth and discovered that someone had already mined all the gold in there. "Take'n ever damned crown in his mouth. After I'd done gone to the trouble of gettin' in there, in the process bustin' the hinges of his jaws, that really pissed me off. And I know who done it too. His sorry-ass son, that got to him before he'd even stiffened up. Done it behind the closed doors of a hospital room. I tell you, there's some real scum in this life . . . ."

I guess the strangest story of Herbert's was one he told me one day while we were breaking for a late lunch from a foundation-leveling job I agreed to help him with. We were both dreadfully filthy from crawling around under a house, jacking up beams and shoring and shimming, and worn out as well, so he declared the job over for the day. We'd crawl back under there the next morning and finish while we were fresh.

"And clean," I reminded him.

"Yeah, you definitely wanna be clean."

Our backs against an enormous oak, whose shade kept us as cool as we were likely to be outside in July in West Texas in the middle of the afternoon, he closed his eyes and began.

"I was a slave once."

Well, that sort of thing will get a guy's attention in a hurry. I set my co-cola down and leaned and looked around the tree at him.

"What do you mean, a slave? You're not even black."

"Don't have to be a nigger to be a slave. I was a old white woman's slave for fourteen years, back when I was young. Did everthang she wanted done on the place and never got paid a red cent for it. Lived in a shack not much bigger'n one of them bedrooms in there." He pointed to the house we'd been working under.

I just kept quiet and let him talk.

What happened was that Herbert was mowing an old woman's yard one day back when he was fresh out of high school and with no particular direction in his life and doing all sorts of odd jobs to get by. He was still living with his folks but didn't get along well with his daddy, so what he wanted most of all was to have enough money to rent a place of his own.

When he had finished the yard, he went to the back door to be paid his dollar, usually a tight, damp cud-like wad that the old lady took from a little leather bag on a string that dangled down from her neck and hung somewhere "amongst her bosoms," as he put it. He'd press it out on his pants leg and put it in his wallet. Only that particular day she didn't fish the bill out. She crooked her finger at him and motioned him into the house and told him to sit down at the kitchen table, which he did. Right then and there she offered him a deal.

"What it was was that she said she'd make me the benafisharary of her will if I would move into the shack out back and do everthang that needed to be done around the place—anythang that come up, you see. Keep her old truck runnin', drive her around wherever she wanted to go, paint stuff, do plumbin' and 'lectrical work, gardenin', carpenter work, just everthang she needed done.

"My eyes snapped, and I knew she knew what was spinnin' around in my head behind'm—she wanted other kind of services too. She up and told me straight out that she didn't want no man like that. I gotta tell you how glad I was to hear it. She must've weighed nearly a quarter-ton and had that lard-gone-bad smell to'r, like lots of old fat white women. That would of killed the deal right there.

"Told me she figured she didn't have long to live and that I'd get everthang she had in the bank, plus the truck and house and furniture and land, which would come to a right smart over $200,000. She showed me the bank statements and everthang, proved she had plenty. Said she'd have the will drawed up immediately and cut her two kids out, since they never come around anyhow, except when they wanted to borry some money off of her. And she showed me a copy of the will the day she had it drawed up. It was there in black and white. I was to get everthang, right down to the plates in the kitchen."

The sun was moving on over in the sky and I wanted to get back to Segovia, but that story had me pretty well nailed to the spot. He talked and I listened, each of us staring off into the distance in different directions.

So for nearly fifteen years he lived on the place and did everything he was asked or ordered to do, accepting what little cash allowance she permitted him, eating at her table, and sleeping on his narrow bed in something approaching squalor. Nights he dreamed of his kingdom to come, and he spent every daydream imagining what he would do when she died.

"I was a slave." He sighed and lit a crooked cigarette from a pack he fished out of a dusty pocket and held it to his lips with the two fingers of his right hand. "For over fourteen damn years handrunnin'."

I didn't want to ask it, but finally I had to: "So what happened? I mean, surely you haven't blown off nearly a quarter of a million dollars."

"Can't blow off what you never got."

When the old woman died, he said, the children showed up "before her body had cooled off" and immediately started hauling stuff away, though he protested violently and threatened to bring the Law in, which eventually he did. But their lawyer made fast work of his objections, completely ignoring him and denying the existence of the will Herbert kept raving about. He had no money to hire an attorney himself and could in no way prove the existence of the will that he had seen with his very own eyes. The will that was unearthed, prepared years before her deal with him, mentioned Herbert not at all.

I leaned around the tree again and looked at his profile against the distant woods. He looked eighty years old, though I doubt that he was fifty, and he had tears in his eyes. Anger maybe, maybe disappointment, maybe just resignation. Whatever, he was crying.

"I've been meaning to ask you something," I said to him.

"You've asked enough questions today."

"Just one more."

"Just one." He wiped his face with his shirt sleeve and left a smear of dirt under his eyes.

"OK." I pointed to the hand that held the cigarette, which he'd smoked down into the filter. "I always wanted to know, how did you lose those two fingers?"

He held his hand out and studied the little stubs, which looked like button mushrooms. "They got bit off."

"What . . . ."

He gave me a look. "No more questions, remember?"

"But . . . ."

That was it, though. I never did find out what bit off the fingers of the only slave I ever knew.

The Pig Thief

For over thirty years, Billy Wayne Stevens lived a perfectly normal Christian life, complete with wife and four kids and, at last count, five grandchildren, even serving for over a decade as a deacon in his church just outside Junction. (I have changed his name to protect him from the certain embarrassment he would suffer were his true identity to become known after what I am about to tell on him.)

It seems that a few weeks ago a knock came at the door, and when Billy Wayne opened it, he beheld two sheriff's deputies with papers of some sort and their hands on their butts (of their pistols, that is), ready for whatever action might be required to take this wicked man back into custody.

For you see, Billy Wayne was a fugitive, having walked off a work gang back in Huntsville in the early seventies after serving eight years of a twenty-year sentence for stealing two dozen pigs. The judge initially sentenced him to a year for each of the purloined pigs, a fairly standard sentence back then, designed to discourage such rustling, but the spirit of the approaching Christmas season was upon him, so he rounded down to an even twenty. Billy could have bartered a bit with the man he stole the swine from, except that he took the pigs to begin with because he didn't have any money, so he didn't have a whole lot to bargain *with* and had to accept his sentence. He did offer a broken-down mule as consolation, but the offended farmer knew the condition of Billy's mule and had already sold his own and bought a tractor and gone modern, so he declined without so much as musing on it a single moment.

After his *excape*, as he pronounces it, Billy Wayne returned to his wife and two small children and moved them swiftly to Fort Stockton, where he began selling used cars, and even without becoming crooked, within five years he had amassed enough cash to afford to buy a small house there in Junction, sufficiently far from the little East Texas town of Groveton, where he'd been convicted, to feel secure in his new life.

And secure he was for all these many years, taking a job at a hardware store in town and becoming a model citizen in every respect that matters, until that knock on the door. Some sorry scumbucket (as he put it) he knew in prison was passing through and recognized him and turned him in.

A few weeks ago I was out that way and decided to drop by and talk with Billy, since I had read about his case in *The Eagle* and found it unusual, if not cruel, that the authorities intended to ignore three decades of clean life and throw him back in the pen to serve out his last twelve pigs, with ten more years tacked on for escaping.

"It don't seem fair to me," he said, as we sipped tea in lawn chairs in his carport. I asked for a beer, but Billy doesn't drink any kind of alcohol or smoke or even swear any harder than something like, "I swan," which I've heard all my life but still don't know the meaning or origin of.

"If I'd of stole some horses or cows, I could see it. That's be rustlin', which in Texas is still purty close to a hangin' offense, but I ain't ever heard pig stealin' called rustlin'. Have you? I mean, they'd have a right to hang my ass if I stole a horse or cow. But that's a whole lot more seriousness about pigs than I ever woulda thought."

I shrugged and said, "I guess it's like all those kids who got busted for half a joint of grass back when the drug laws were so tough and ended up serving more time than they would have if they had hacked their mommas to death with a hoe. Just different times, different kind of justice. Less tolerance."

"At's a fact," he said.

"Why, today you could steal the equivalent weight in vacuum-sealed tenderloins and bacon and not get fifteen years. Four at most, I'd say, but more like two. Of course you probably wouldn't even get caught, since they would never squeal on you."

He didn't see a whole lot of humor in that, so I was a little sorry about it and told him so, and he said it was OK, that he had pretty well lost his sense of humor.

"Do you eat pork?" I asked him, then realized that he might think I was making fun of him. But you know how it is when you know better than to ask somebody something but you just have to do it anyway?

He gave me a really hard look. "I ain't so much as touched a fork to anything that come off a pig since I excaped. I eat sausage and bacon and ham while I was in, because I figgered I had earned it. I ain't had a thing to do with pigs since then. Ours is what I call a hogless home."

His lawyer feels pretty confident that he can win before a jury, given Billy's long tenure of right-eousness, but prosecutors seem equally certain that the pigs will be worked off in full, plus ten years. Were that to be the case, he would be a very old man before he walks away from the pen again.

I asked him why he stole the pigs to begin with, what was he going to do with a whole herd of hogs, and he said that he really stole just one, a shoat, but it must have been a favorite of the bunch because as he was walking down the road with it in his arms, it squealing its little head off, he looked behind him and the whole lot was following him home, which is how he got caught. You might spirit off one little pig in your arms, leaving no hoofprints, and hide it properly, but a blind man in a wheelchair could have followed that hog trail that led right to his house.

"They had me in custody before I had time to explain to my wife how come all them hogs was gathered in the yard."

Word is the church is praying really hard for Billy Wayne and taking a special collection every Sunday for his defense fund. They even had a bake sale to raise money for him, and a host of kind folks raised the money for his bail.

His case is coming up in early January, so soon he'll know the true price for bringing home the bacon. Meanwhile he dutifully goes to work each and day and attends church regularly and steadfastly refuses pork. A fine man is Billy Wayne Stevens, and I am rooting for him.

Bobby Wayne Learns a Thanksgiving Lesson

This story was told me by Dr. Walter York-shire Mason, retired physician, who settled along the river at Segovia some ten years ago not far from where he grew up, having found even the sparsely traveled streets of Kerrville a bit too busy for his blood.

It was on a Thanksgiving some twenty years ago, and all was well upon the hill where three generations of the Mason clan had gathered at the family ancestral home, a sprawling ranch house above the river valley, but for a problem with Bobby Wayne, shining child of his doting parents but a steadfast thorn in the side of the female cousins. (It is amazing how many boys and men with the middle name *Wayne* get in trouble.)

Having reached the age of fifteen alive and barely scarred, Bobby behaved as if he knew no wrath could fall upon him that his smile and pale blue eyes would not render helpless. And so it was that when he crossed the lines of staunch decorum, little was done to set him straight, this single son with no sister.

"It is only Bobby Wayne being a boy," his father would say, proud of his fine lineage.

"Just Bobby Wayne," his mom agreed, stroking his blond hair and placing a kiss upon his cherubic cheek.

Bobby was the only boy among the grandchildren, and he rode this distinction hard and heavy, falling so soundly into the graces of Grandpa and Grandma Mason that they brushed his little indiscretions off like flies and shooed them hither, assigning him his own room in their house, the only grandchild so graced. And the aunts and uncles loved him too, this blond and blue-eyed prince. "Just a boy," they said. A thorn he was to the girls, but one the others gladly suffered. Who knew what he might grow into?

Ah, but Bobby was far from a favorite among the lithe and lovely cousins. Three of them there were this time—Molly, Brenda, and Sarah—one with long black tresses, two lighter-haired sisters, the other two electing not to come and have to deal with Bobby Wayne, so great was this scourge upon them.

Alas, they were not even near Turkey Time when Bobby Wayne laid his hand on a place on Molly that out of simple civility shall go unnamed— but for purposes of minimal identification, these places come in pairs on the human female, up front and high on their anatomy. The four of them were sitting in the barn loft playing Scrabble on a table made of a bale of hay when Bobby reached across the board and touched what he little understood but knew he must be fond of in order to be a Big Boy. Molly squealed, but not from pleasure, and knocked his hand away and scurried down the ladder and retreated from the scene, whereupon Bobby turned his attention to the sisters, using every word he'd ever heard that he thought might nigh impress them and pinning Sarah against the straw until she wiggled loose and followed Brenda down the ladder.

This time it was, as they say, the last straw for the girls. They ran and hid behind the house until Bobby shambled down toward the creek to throw rocks at turtles, then went back to the loft and put their pretty heads together, one of raven hair, two of tawny, and alas, a plan was born whereby Bobby might be dealt with.

The grandest folly of the male is to underestimate the female, at all levels, as he is wont to do. Bobby Wayne Mason had had his way with the lovely cousins so long, lording it over them, touching as he would, saying what he liked, that not even the strayest of notions that he might have a price to pay ventured into his largely vacant head. This is too often the case for a boy, blessed as he is with an intellect that should set him well above the hooved and horned and hairy, but with an arrogance and hormonal rage that drives all wisdom from him.

So there was Bobby Wayne Mason strutting up the hedged drive of the old homeplace, not a quarter of a mile from the new, in search of the female cousins, known to gather in the weathered house once for games and little parties involving tea and dolls but now for talk of boys. And he was, after all, BOY, almost MAN, cousin or not, and in his head strange notions danced from ear to ear. He had felt faint stirrings above and below, now gathered to greatness in him, a surge to be obeyed rather than allayed. So he would act upon them.

Ah, but Bobby Wayne knew not what dreadful fate awaited him. He had crossed the cousins a time too many, and now he must be punished, only how could he know this, being swamped by hormones and bereft of common sense?

"Oh, Bobby Wayne, Bobby Wayne," a voice came from out the hedge, low and sweet and thrilling, smooth as panty silk and soft as summer butter, "would you like to see me now with all my clothes from off me and touch my you-know-what, sir?"

What boy or man could resist this call, cousin or not, sir? Bobby dove into the hedge, like plunging into water, and found himself enjungled there—six sets of claws unsheathed, three mouths howling, three racks of fangs upon him.

And when at last he surfaced, a shocked and trembling thing, weak and mewling like a baby—striated, torn, and bleeding—his pride stripped bare of what it was, ravaged soul and body, poor Bobby limped off to his room and huddled there, resisting all entreaties, though the sun passed across the sky and settled westward red and swollen. Word was he had gotten lost in a great patch of briars and endured a terrible shredding.

Next day, as the others talked and watched TV and surfeited on Thanksgiving plenty, Bobby Wayne lay sullen in his room while across his window dashed the girls, shrieking gaily, "Catch us, Bobby, if you can, and you may be our master. We are but little Gypsy girls, harmless as the wind and ripe now to be taken."

Poor Bobby winced at their cries and wept and snuffled—forlorn, ashamed, and shaken.

The boy grew up to become a successful county politician, with dreams of ascending to the legislature, and word is that to this day when he is around the female cousins, now broadening into middle-age, with many children of their own, he treats them with utmost respect and the reverence that is due them. So sayeth the good doctor.

Booger Estes and the Windfall

When Booger Estes, resident of Segovia, was notified by registered letter that he was to be the recipient of the better part of his deceased Aunt Audrey's estate, he being her favorite nephew and the only one with what she judged to have even a modicum of common sense about him, he sat a long time on an inverted five-gallon paint bucket out behind his small tractor shed and pondered the direction that his future might take when at long last what was left of the lawyer-devastated inheritance reached his mailbox or was delivered unto him for signing and rendering into cash.

His parents died paupers, when a train ran flat over their pickup, and left him with less in assets than what they owed, and he, honest and upright American that he was and is, refused to sue the railroad—which he might well have done, since the engineer was drunk at the levers, seven different lawyers wearing grooves in his porch steps to tell him so—and chose instead to work hard over nearly a decade to pay off their debts. This he did willingly, and he smiled with satisfaction when he folded the last *paid in full* receipt and stuffed it into his wallet.

The following Sunday, after making a copy of the receipt, he buried the original in a little jelly jar between the plots where his folks lay in their eternal sleep, knowing that they would sleep even better now that they were square with the world.

Two months to the day after he was notified of his windfall, a check did arrive in the mail, made out to Booger—though in his real name, Oscar Samuel Estes—in the sum of $8457.42. He never knew how much it was before the lawyers laid into it, since such figures are kept confidential. This amount he deposited in his checking account before sundown that day, minus $457.42. He liked nice round numbers like $8000 to enter into his checkbook, and nearly $500 worth of twenties gave his wallet a wondrous swell that he had not sat upon in all of his life of nearly fifty years except once when he got a hip hematoma from falling off a ladder onto his butt. (He noticed often that wealthy men sat a little lopsided, and probably not from hematomas.) He left the bank a decidedly happy man.

But happiness is seldom long lasting for the newly wealthy, since wealth begets the desire for more wealth and spawns the fear of losing what wealth you have, and so it was that the day after his mammoth deposit he found himself once again seated on the paint can behind his tractor shed wondering how he might ratchet his windfall into double or triple what Aunt Audrey had left in his charge, for this she would expect—at least this, if nothing more. He sat long and pondered, swept up in the misery that only the heritor can know. Not even his small acreage, green with June corn, whose golden tassels waved to him like friendly neighbors, and rows and rows of peas and beans, appealed to him now, nor Earlene, his Bluetick Hound of fifteen years, who lay beside him, on her back, ready for a rubbing.

It was not that he doubted his ability to do something wise with the money. He was known throughout the county as something of an experimenter, though not necessarily a wise one. Once when someone told him why his Aunt Bertha's porch ceiling back in Huntsville was painted blue, so that wasps would not build nests there and flies would not land, he brushed his entire herd of eight heifers Powdery Birdsegg (from Sherman Williams, as he put it) to keep off the flies, but the ASPCA came down on him like a caboose when most of the ungulates' hair fell out and the flies were worse than ever, though he did point out to all interested parties that he never had to knock a wasp nest off a single cow.

And he theorized once that the way to make a fortune in hamburgers was to add food coloring to the meat and offer what he called Booger's Rainbow Burgers, so he took his meager savings, earned by a couple of good corn and sweet potato crops, and late one fall (after harvest was complete) opened a small joint called Booger's Burgers out near the interstate. But within three calendar months, the only kind he ever knew, all his money was gone, people having snubbed such offerings as Booger's Red-Hot, Spinach-Green, Sea-Blue, and Meller-Yeller in favor of the dull, grayish-brown patties other burger places peddled. He was back to farming full-time in the spring.

Once he'd scrounged up another little wad of cash, he approached his Aunt Beulah, the one with the goiter and what she called a prescription to *Money Magazine*, and asked her about mutual funds, but she argued that they were merely a form of government-sanctioned communism and suggested he let her borrow the money to have the goiter removed, promising him a ten percent return on his money. And this he agreed to, only to discover that Beulah not only couldn't afford to pay back the principal of the loan—she couldn't even pay the interest. He was out his money and Beulah was out her goiter, so he wrote it off as even and turned to his affairs as if he'd never had the money to begin with, and he bore no lasting ill will toward Beulah. A few Sundays of her fried ground squirrel and shoepeg-corn casserole assured that, especially since he no longer had to look across the table and wonder at the nature of the goiter—from whence it came, and what it felt like to carry one.

So it was that Booger Estes, after many a mile of pondering, if thoughts could be measured in linear fashion, decided that the thing to do was get in his pickup and drive over to Kerrville and see whether he could run across anything that might trigger a plan.

This he did. He slowly drove up and down every street that had a trace of commercialism on it, even the highways leading in and out, and lo and behold, before the afternoon was out his eyes and heart were literally afire with entrepreneurial zeal.

Two weeks later he had knocked down every cross-fence on the place and bushhogged the corn and peas and beans and made one vast fifty-acre pasture, the sum of his holdings except for the little corner his trailer and outbuildings squatted on, and sold the thirteen mixed heifers and two bull calves that made up his herd. By sundown of the day after disposing of his cows, Booger Estes was the proud owner of twenty-two Black Angus heifers and one runty but certifiably viable Angus bull.

As he sat in his metal spring-legged lawn chair on the deck behind his trailer, he proudly studied his new acquisition while the herd moved slowly across the rows of flattened corn and peas and beans, fattening for the day when they would fetch a pretty penny at the local auction, bound for Kroger and Wal-mart meat counters and all the burger places listing Angus among their many offerings. The old lawn chair squawked as he leaned back and sighed, content that for once he had reasoned wisely and well and Aunt Audrey would be proud.

"Angus," he whispered softly to the settling dark, "is in."

The Tale of Tank Murdock

Tank Murdock got his name at a very early age, having come into this world at something over a dozen pounds and doing nothing after that but fulfilling his destiny: to become a most notable specimen of mankind. By the age of twelve he weighed over two hundred pounds and stood well over six feet.

It was, then, with no small degree of delight that his friends and schoolmates derided him for his bulk, though none would make fun of him to his face, fearing that should he decide to descend upon them, nothing would save them from a squashing.

For a child of such tonnage, there is little else to do than pretend that you are normal and go about your life as anyone else might, whether or not you are aware that you create a fair representation of an eclipse when you walk between other children and the sun. Tank smiled and tried to befriend all, large and small, and usually he succeeded.

By the time he was in his junior-high years he topped the scales at three hundred pounds, making him the object of both ridicule and awe. Those who liked him loved to hover in his shadow, and those who feared or disliked him laughed and pointed but steered clear of that massive mountain of flesh. Tank did not care: He was simply Tank to all, near and far, big and small.

In time he became dearer and dearer to all who knew him, lovable leviathan that he was, and it was seldom that he was without a throng of friends. When there was a party, Tank was there, and when he was there, there were never leftovers. When mischief was afoot, Tank was there, since in his eagerness to be a friend to everyone, he would fall in with the wrong crowd just as quickly as he did with the right.

One moonless October night when boredom had totally erased any trace of sense in the minds of those involved, a covey of six boys, including Tank, decided to drive about and smash mailboxes on the rural routes with a baseball bat, the barrel hollowed out and packed with lead shot and sealed with epoxy to give it adequate heft. One good swing and a mailbox would crumple like a beer can in the hand of a Southern roofer, sometimes shear off its mounting and tumble end over end, coming to rest yards down the road. On a good night as many as thirty boxes might bite the dust. Oh, what a splendid game it was to these vacuous sons of the South.

Thing was, when it came Tank's time at the bat that night, all aboard miscalculated his breadth so that when he leaned out and drew back to send a mailbox into low-earth orbit, he was wedged too resolutely to make an adjustment when Earl Talbert, who was driving the car, came a bit too close so that the mailbox was high and inside and before Tank could bring the bat around, his head struck and smashed it just as decidedly as that bat would have done, leaving the young man quite addled, but not so much so that he lost his grip on the bat, which was all the others were worried about. The loss of a Louisville Slugger packed with lead was worse than losing Tank's head.

They managed to get Tank back home alive that night, his swollen head wrapped in a pair of pantyhose Earl remembered that he had in the trunk and that he loved to tell the story about how they got there, and the boy showered and went to bed and his parents were none the wiser for his folly, though for days afterwards he spoke hesitantly, if at all.

His injury was such that Tank slipped low in academics—well, lower than he had been, say from a C- student to something south of F—but swelled in girth until when he walked down the hall between classes, students heading toward him parted like a stream around a vast boulder, a fact that the principal, Mr. John Turner, also the head football coach, took note of and acted swiftly on, being the shrewd man that he was.

One morning in late May Mr. Turner summoned Tank, a fact that frightened the boy into a heavy sweat as he slouched down to the principal's office.

When Tank entered the office, Coach Turner, as he preferred to be called, backed the lad against the wall and took out a tape measure and calculated precisely how much space he would take up in a football line.

"Right at three feet," he muttered, "and I ain't talking circumference." Since he did some double duty as a math teacher, he knew the difference between circumference and diameter and radii and all that.

"How far and fast could you run if they was to be a bear on your ass?" he asked Tank.

"I figger he'd get me right off," the boy replied. "I guess I'd have to fight him."

"But I'm asking you how far could you get before he take'n you down?"

"Maybe six or eight steps, if it was a big bear. Maybe ten if it was medium-size. And I ain't so sure that a bear could do it, without he was *real* big."

"And exactly how much experience have you had fightin' bears, Son?"

"None. Ain't ever seen a bear in person."

"But you think you could *whip* one?"

"Well, sir, like I said, if he wudn't *real* big. I turned a Volkswagen over on its side one time. And one time I wrestled a bull that weighed over a ton, and I would have pinned him, except I broke off one of his horns. I figger I could give most bears a purty good fight."

Coach Turner studied him a few minutes, then nodded. "That'll do. You ain't ever gon' make grades worth a bear's *ass*, but you are gon' play football. We might have to get you some shoulder pads made out of giant sea turtle shells or somethin' and make you a uniform out of bulk canvas, but, by God, you gon' play football."

So it was that Tank Murdock became the anchor man in the offensive and defensive lines of the varsity football team, Coach Turner having reasoned that here was a magnitude of flesh that could well serve to prevent any offensive plays up the middle and totally ward off any defensive rush against his quarterback. All Tank had to do was drop into a three-point stance, then rise and drive forward and crush to the ground anybody trying to block him, forcing the play to one end or the other but never up the middle and scaring the squirts out of any quarterback watching that mass lumbering toward him, or, with his log-like arms spread, prevent nearly eight feet of defensive line from penetrating the zone behind him, thereby allowing the rest of the defensive line to concentrate on the players Tank didn't mow down.

In practice, when the other players were running sprints or slamming into the sleds or knocking each other senseless in close-quarter drills, all

Tank had to do was work on his three-point stance and surge. He would drop down, feet planted, the knuckles of one hand on the ground, then rise up and take five or six lumbering steps forward, then back up and do it again. Once they brought in a mule that belonged to Carl Waldrop and let Tank catch him broadside. He broke three of the mule's ribs, and it took half the team to get the animal back on its feet. Carl said the mule never cared for football again, would, in fact, go and quiver in the corner of the lot when any of the kids started throwing a ball around. The Coach figured that Tank would never need to move more than three or four yards forward and that nothing short of a nuclear blast would move him backwards.

The upshot is that that year and for the next two Coach Turner's team won the district title, largely because of Tank Murdock, who rarely broke a sweat but broke four legs, seven arms, two jaws, and racks and racks of ribs of players on opposing teams. He was a force to be reckoned with, almost of Biblical proportions.

But even ol' Tank had eventually to graduate, and this he did, through the collective efforts of Principal Turner and a gaggle of his teachers.

After graduation, Tank briefly entertained the notion of seeking a football scholarship at a local junior college, but since he had the agility of a concrete bunker, the coaches he contacted shook their heads and dismissed him. So it was that he entered the work force as a stocker at a Wal-Mart, but the job lasted only long enough for him to tumble off a ladder and onto an elderly lady cruising beneath him in a motorized cart, rendering both her and the cart quite beyond repair. The settlement that followed sealed his fate with the company, and he found himself jobless, with few prospects for employment, and living off his folks, a heavy burden for them, given his ability to graze through groceries with the zeal of a storm of locusts.

Well, Tank did what desperate people often do: He turned to a preacher. He had attended a nearby Protestant church—I am very carefully avoiding hinging this on any particular denomination, you understand, out of fear of offending anyone—with his parents almost all his life, so it was only natural that he would consult Reverend Ponds, himself at one time rotund, though in no manner approaching the magnitude of Tank's girth. The Reverend had over a space of several months shed some eighty pounds of unneeded bulk, and though he did not have a lean and hungry look, he was half the eclipse he used to be when he walked down the aisle at Sunday morning service.

When Tank and Brother Ponds met for their first session in a series designed to help this poor wayward mountain of a boy find his path through the world's perilous thicket, the first thing the Reverend said was, "Son, you have to lose about half of yourself before you can hope to be employed in any position outside the circus."

He was not being unkind, only serious, and Tank simply asked, "How I'm gon' do that, since I ain't done a thang but put on pounds since I come out of Momma?"

"By follerin' the program I do, Son: the Hallelujah Diet."

They were in the preacher's church office. Brother Ponds rose from his desk and took a folder out of a file cabinet. He flipped through some papers and then laid one on the desk.

"Whussat?" the boy asked him.

"It is a plan to where by follerin' the dictates of the Bible and eatin' the foods prescribed therein, you might shuck off a hunderd pounds in just a matter of months."

To which Tank replied that he had tried everything under the sun to whittle off excess weight but didn't even manage to slow down the accumulation.

To which Reverend Ponds, who had resumed his seat behind the desk, replied, "This here's a different approach, and I'll guarantee you it'll work. What you do is eat what the Bible talks about God's chosen a-eatin': fruits and nuts and seeds and stuff like that, and . . ."

"But the Bible's got goats and jackasses and whales in it too," Tank said.

"Them's God's *livin'* creatures, and you cannot eat them. You cannot rend and chew and swaller *flesh*, Son. It ain't permitted. Or eat sugar and animal fats and processed bread. You can't gnaw on nuthin' but fruits and seeds and nuts and honey, like is described in the Bible. If you foller my plan, you will shuck off two hunderd pounds by Christmas." He looked at the calendar on his desk. "This *comin'* Christmas, right at eight months."

"But we don't eat *live* animals. We kill'm first. Or at least I never eat a live one, and I don't intend to."

Brother Ponds gave him a stern look. "So you figger it's any righter to kill one of God's creatures before you eat him? Son, listen to yerself! If you eat a animal, it has got to be killed first, or you generally got a purty good fight on your hands. You *eat* it, somebody's got to kill it first, and that makes you a accessory to the crime, because that animal wouldn't of been killed without there was somebody wantin' to eat him."

"OK, then, what about *fish*, which Jesus divided up and fed to the multitudes?"

"Them fish was a metaphor. They wudn't real fish, just manna in the *shape* of fish."

"But some of the prophets—"

"Son, are you listenin' to me or not?"

"Yessir. OK, then, what about ice cream? And Skittles?"

"Son, where in the Bible is they any mention of ice cream and Skittles, whatever the hell—whatever that is? No dairy products. They come from God's livin' creatures." He slid the sheet of paper over to Tank. "Take this list that'll tell you what is and is not forbidden."

The boy nodded his head and said simply, "Yessir. I'll try. But I 'mon find it real hard to give up meat and ice cream and Skittles and stuff like that."

The upshot is that Tank came away from that first meeting with the pastor and followed religiously the two-page set of instructions that outlined what he could and could not eat on the Hallelujah Diet, and within a month he had dropped forty pounds. In two months he had left nearly eighty pounds somewhere. By Christmas he had indeed dumped two hundred pounds and could buy his clothes and belts from places like J.C. Penney and Sears.

But much more importantly, our young man Tank, now a tankette, had rolled all his peasant cunning into a tight little ball of conviction: that what had shucked the weight off him would work for anybody. All he had to do was come up with a plan whereby he might profit from what had been given him free by Brother Ponds. And this he did.

Today, on a hilltop not far from the Segovia Truck Stop, there is a cluster of buildings at the end of a winding road, and down on the highway at the base of that road is a sign with an arrow pointing up the hill. It reads: *Hallelujah Heaven: Where You Can Have Your Funnage While you Lose Your Tonnage.* And the lord of the hill is our own Tank Murdock, proud owner of Hallelujah Heaven.

There you may go and spend anywhere from

two weeks to a year, depending on how much weight you wish to lose, and from a thousand dollars to tens of thousands, depending on how much you have to lose and how badly you want to lose it. Nothing in the way of nourishment is allowed on the place except the Biblical food that Tank has approved, much of which he grows himself on some small acreage behind the massive dining hall, where residents are served six meals a day. Once the gates close on a customer, he may not leave until his time is up. Vehicles are parked at the foot of the hill in a guarded lot, and customers are carried up to the Administration Building in a school bus, painted white and with HALLELUJAH HEAVEN in bold blue letters on both sides and below it the painting of a cornucopia, out of which spill olives and barley sprigs and fruits, nuts, and vegetables of every sort. Dotting the hillside are cottages in which residents live out their time at Hallelujah Heaven.

When I last spoke with Tank, he announced that he had added a lap pool, double-wide to accommodate the broadest of those who come to him, and built a tennis court next to the recreational hall. He has a great range of entertainment for his guests, so that everyone but the pathologically bored will have "funnage while losing their tonnage." A final touch: Above the sign down on the highway he has erected an electronic counter that tabulates the total pounds lost to that point during the year, presently 2212 and counting, or roughly, he says, "thirteen average-size people, and we didn't even have to berry'm or burn'm."

So there you have it: another little American success story. No matter what hand you are dealt in life, play it right and you'll come out a winner every time.

Returning to Segovia: a Story

Tattered Coat Upon a Stick

**"An aged man is but a paltry thing,
A tattered coat upon a stick, unless
Soul clap its hands and sing, and louder sing
For every tatter in its mortal dress . . ."
("Sailing to Byzantium," William Butler Yeats)**

They must have assumed him deaf or asleep, the way they allowed their voices to drift down the hallway to where he lay in his granddaughter's bed waiting for the night to come. He had already had his medicine for the evening, could feel it easing over his body like warm oil. From outside came sounds of the city—whizzing cars and blaring horns, and somewhere far off the wail of a crossing train. Or perhaps they did not care that he heard.

And what he heard, whether they intended or not, was the same message that had come to him clearly enough over the weeks since his last hospital visit, when doctors pumped fluid off his lungs the third time and told the children that with his next admission he probably wouldn't be going home alive.

Through gentle attempts at persuasion, then ardent confrontation, he was advised that when his time came, the body would be placed next to their mother's in her family's plot in Tyler, properly and with much grace and dignity, the way people were meant to be tucked away for eternity. In a place where he could be diligently cared for over the years, flowers refreshed, grass clipped, and the stone kept clear of vines and creeping moss, a place where someday they would all lie together in a row, father and mother and three children, the way it was intended, orderly and neat and with room enough for spouses and the grandchildren, should they in their time choose to follow. He remembered from his few trips there that it was a large hillside plot, shady and pleasant, but it was not where he wanted to take his eternal rest.

It was not something he wanted to talk about, this matter of being disposed of. What man does? But when it was obvious that the subject had to be faced, he did.

"It seems to me," he had said to them the evening after doctors told the family he would not last out the year, "a man's final place is his to choose. He's got no word on coming into this world, but he ought to have the right to an opinion on the way out. He earns that right by living."

Seated about him the living room, his two sons and a daughter, themselves now well into middle age, merely looked sad and shook their heads. "By suffering through raising children!" he boomed, rising before them and weaving on unsteady legs toward the door.

"It is not *right*," one of the sons came back, "it's against all that is proper and civilized, being burned, then scooped up like something from a stove and scattered in that Godforsaken wasteland out there where it never rains and nothing grows but cactus and mesquite. Where nobody'll ever visit your grave and put flowers on it. Where there won't even *be* a grave. When you could be buried in that historical cemetery, right next to Momma."

"Where everything's lush and green," the other son added.

He spun around and braced himself in the doorway, his face fierce. "I never lived in Tyler, never spent a full day of my life in Tyler, and I don't intend to spend enternity there, even if that Goddamned plot *is* paid for. That's *her* family plot, not mine. It has never been any of mine. Where I have spent a good part of my life and the best is out there at the ranch, which y'all call a wasteland. And it is mine, bought and paid for a long ago and held through the toughest of times by men stronger than you will ever be. Well, what is a wasteland to you is paradise to me, and what you apparently regard as paradise is a piece of city real estate cared for by people who don't give a *damn* about who's buried there. *Plastic flowers.* At least what grows around the graves out there is real—curly mesquite or buffalo grass or cactus. It's *real.* It's what I love, that place out there, and it's where I want to spend eternity, what's left of me. And it is *my* choice!" He shook a pale fist at them and stormed down the hallway, slamming behind him the door to what they called his bedroom in his daughter's suburban Houston home, though he knew as well as they did that it was just a quick stopover, a halfway house to forever.

Now he lay across the bed and studied the opposite wall with its pink floral wallpaper, while down the hall they talked fervently and low and evening settled on the city.

He had long ago decided that he wanted to be cremated and his ashes scattered at the old family place in Segovia, the five-hundred-acre river valley homestead his grandfather and father had held through lean times and flush against drought and flood and banks and he himself lately from wealthy men in Houston looking for land along the river for retirement homes. Except for the financial urgencies of a family with three kids, who had to be fed and clothed and educated properly, he would have spent his entire life out there scratching away at some sort of living, but at least getting by. That's what he had wanted.

It was a raw land, lying at the southern edge of the Edwards Plateau and west of the Texas Hill Country. For miles as one drove west the view seldom changed except for the river valleys, like the one the ranch lay in, where flat, mesquite-studded fields stretched out from banks lined with oak and pecan to the edge of stark bluffs that rose to plateaus covered with patches of cedar and clumps of scrub oak, broken here and there by draws gouged over millenia by water rushing down to the river during winters typically wet. Some oat and barley patches colored the valley until late spring, but when summer set in with its blowtorch sun and long stretches of drought, the most dependable springs drying up in the draws, whatever the hopeful owners planted withered and browned, and the indomitable mesquite reclaimed fields and grew sometimes twice the height of a man before winter forced it into dormancy again. It was a good land only to those who loved and understood it and did not demand more than it could deliver. And it was good to Mitchell Turner, who, though he had not had to earn his living from it, worked many a long hour as a boy helping his grandfather and father keep the family alive with the pitiful bounty it bore.

He had never bothered to explain to anyone why he wanted to keep the place after his mother died and then his father and it passed to him. Over the years there had been offers from affluent men in San Antonio and Houston who wanted to erect game fences around the entire ranch and introduce new breeds of exotics for city hunters, but he steadfastly refused, allowing only a handful of men he knew personally to come onto the place in the fall and winter to take sika and axis bucks from the herds that fed along the river and bedded in the draws.

What he took in from the hunters did little more than pay the taxes on the property and utilities for the house, which still stood like a great stone fortress after over a century of West Texas weather. A sheepman leased the place all year, paying so small a fee that he might just as well not pay anything at all, but the sheep did keep the place clipped over, closer than a mower could manage, persistent and without noise.

Even as a man well over seventy he made frequent trips out from his Houston home, built in the western suburbs forty years before when, as a fast-rising oil-patch engineer, he needed to be near his job, and his wife wanted to live in the sort of house she believed engineers' wives ought to have. He had never liked the city, but they had raised the kids there and it was a good enough home away from home, the ranch only five hours due west, an easy drive, interstate almost all the way. He had spent a couple of weeks each summer and a week at Christmas break and at least two weekends a month out there all his adult life. Until the cancer was diagnosed.

What he did while he was at the ranch was nothing special. He fixed pipes when they broke or clogged with mineral scale, patched the roof, painted now and again, and did all the little chores required to keep the house in shape and fences from falling down. Three or four trips out each year would have sufficed for maintenance, especially with his sheepman coming by to check on the property every week. Each fall he paid a neighbor to break the oat patches, tearing out by the roots young mesquite shrubs that swarmed out from field edge with the massive heat of summer, and plant winter forage for deer. Every couple of years he gathered branches and cut up dead trees on the hill tops and stacked them for burning after they had seasoned.

It was being there that mattered, not what he did while he was there. His psyche seemed aligned once again the minute he passed the iron gate, like a spinning compass needle settling straight and true on north, and it remained stable for days after he left. It was therapy for him, just walking around and piddling and remembering, and all it cost him was a manageable gas bill and occasional discord with the family. A great while ago they would often accompany him, the whole family, and after the children were grown sometimes just his wife, but usually he went alone.

As he aged, the trips seemed even more urgent, as if he had started reading a very long book that he feared he might not finish before death stopped the story, and he could not wait until retirement, when it was his full intention to move out to the ranch, with or without his wife. But when that time finally came, she refused any notion of moving out there, and she made it clear that if he went, it would mean the end of the marriage. She would not live in such isolation, she told him—if he wanted to make a go of it on his own out there, he could do it without her, but he would find her doors locked to him when he made up his mind to come home. She was unrelenting.

So after he retired, he continued for years to make his weekend trips, occasionally with his wife but usually alone, and the whole family met out there July 4th weekend, spent a couple of days at Thanksgiving, and often stayed a week at Christmas. Only *he* truly enjoyed being out there, a fact made clear by each of the others from time to time, including his wife, but he insisted on honoring the tradition until her illness made the family gatherings impossible. After her death, but for a couple of hunting trips a year with the boys, he was the only one who kept going out.

His initial diagnosis led to months of treatment during which he was reassured by physicians that his body was gaining lost ground, but he knew his body better than anyone else, and it was telling him to find a place to lie down for good. It knew as a dying animal knows. Find some place of solitude and lie down and wait for the great eternal dark, wait for a season of suns to burn your flesh away and return your atoms to the earth from whence they came. The message was clear.

So he decided to get what was left of his life in order. He sold the Houston house and whatever the children didn't want from the household goods and moved in with his daughter, who in her own way probably loved him more than the sons—at least she tolerated him better than they did. Women were that way. They put up with males at both ends all their lives, wiping little boys' butts, then dabbing saliva off an old man's chin. He'd always said that it paid to have daughters. This one was divorced, with two children who now shared a room, and if he felt comfortable anywhere away from his own home it was with her.

If the boys would back off, he knew he could talk her into letting him have his way about his final dispensation, but they were adamant about fulfilling the promise they'd made their mother that they would all be together, bones intact, in death. Every time he thought about that noisy plot in Tyler tended by a mouth-breathing white trash boy whose teeth looked like walnut shells, he had to go lie down and try to focus on the little shady plot where his father lay.

Now he managed only an occasional visit to the ranch, when one of the kids would take the time to drive him out for a day or two, and twice he went by bus. They were pestering him to sell the land, but he refused. "After I'm gone," he told them, "I don't give a good Goddamn what you do with it. I'll be in it, *part* of it, so it won't matter. I go with the land, no matter *who's* got the paper." They always nodded at each other, lips tight.

His last trip out, he had strange sensations that began when the bus broke out of the clutter of San Antonio and the land stretched out before him, wild and without people but for the occasional ranch house in valleys or grand home on the top of a hill. There seemed to be a spirit hovering, shapeless and without color but as certain as the land itself, and the bus was driving through it. It pressed on all sides, against his face and arms, his chest, and though it caught him breathless, it was strangely comforting.

"Maybe I am dying," he said to himself, "or maybe it is just gladness. Or maybe something I ate." He felt it all the way to the Segovia Truck Stop, and even when he got off the bus and phoned a friend to drive him to the ranch. There, as he stood with the old iron gate flung open and he could see the hills rising behind the clump of trees that hid the homesite, the spirit—whatever it was—lifted and he was himself again.

Even as a quickly aging man he had given little thought to death, preferring to believe that when the time came it would be swift and resolute, as it had been for his father when a heart attack struck him down in a flash as he was cutting a fallen tree into sections for splitting. He fell forward, a man just over sixty, and landed on the revving chain, his finger clenching the throttle wide open. The saw took off half the left side of his face and buried itself into his shoulder and chest. When they got to him, the saw was still running, flinging tissue and bone and blood in a jagged, tawdry line twenty feet out from his father, who was probably dead before he landed on the whirring chain.

With pick and shovel he dug the hole himself, drove the puny little tools into the flank of the hillside and chipped out a depression deep enough to accommodate the simple wooden casket, then built a mound of dirt and stone that had lasted nearly a decade before rain and frost and armadillos worried it level. His father's stone was the fourth in the family plot on the side of the spring draw, cool and shady and green most of the year, tended by nothing but the seasons.

If it had to be, it was enough to seep into the soil of that little plot laid off by a rail fence and stone border. That was compromise enough. But he loved all of it, hill and field, mesquite thickets that led up the the hills, where gnarled oaks and cedars began, the tall, lush hardwoods of the draws, stone and soil blackened by leafmold, the twisting little streams that issued from white rock and lost themselves in deep sand in summer at the edge of the valley floor, and what he really wanted was for the handful of ashes left from purifying fire to be flung off the high cliffs over the oat patches, settling wherever wind and water would carry them, up the hillside and over the fields, all the way to the chortling river.

Now as his body slowly failed him, ravaged by an insidious tumor that spread like the virulent mesquite in summer, he felt an urgency to be done with this untidy business of dying. He wanted a sudden death—a flash in the sun like the blade of the misswung axe that left a long bright scar on his shin—and though his Catholic background had rarely allowed him to think seriously about suicide, as he watched himself ebb slowly, subsiding like a plant withered by frost, he entertained more and more often the notion of dispatching himself quickly. Perhaps sitting in his bathtub at the ranch, if he could manage to get away from them long enough to make his way back out there and get his old pistol, which he always carried for snakes, and shoot himself in the temple. When they found him they could lift his frail, bird-like body, rinse out the tub.

But it all got so *terribly* untidy when he thought about suicide. He wanted to be *cremated*, his ashes scattered across the ranch. He knew deep down he'd never win that argument, because they were stauncher Catholics than ever he had been, he who along with his wife had taught them well the sanctity of the body and the necessity of tradition and ritual in managing it from womb to grave. He would be satisfied enough if they would just *tell* him they would bury him on the Place and make him believe it. But they had also taught the children not to lie. Ah, the human story was such a tale of desolations and disappointments—it was out of his hands and in theirs, the young and strong and more willful.

The notion of cremation never crossed his mind until he found the Indian's grave one cold December day, the sky as gray and soggy as an old blanket thrown away in the trash, a wash of low clouds scudding across the hills and settling in a tight, heavy mist in the bottoms and along slopes of the draws. It was two days before the children would be arriving, one with wife and baby, the other two in from college for the holidays, and his wife had already filled the house with cooking smells that when the wind was right drifted all the way back into the mesquite thickets where he hunted and sometimes to the very tops of the cedar-thick hills.

He was traversing a steep, wooded slope of what he referred to as Hill Number One, the southernmost of three hills formed by deep draws from runoff from the plateaus. They projected straight out into the river valley like three fingers, rising perhaps two hundred feet off the valley floor and covered with thick growth of cedar and scattered scrub oak except in the spring draws, where massive oaks stood with here and there a cottonwood or elm. The draws were a haven for deer, especially exotics—axis and sika and fallow—which fed along the river and adjoining fields, and whitetail roamed the entire place, feeding in the bottomlands with the exotics evenings and mornings but preferring the draws and hills for cover during the day.

This slope, gradually steepening to the edge of a rock-jumbled draw that swept down from the hill almost precisely on the property line between him and his neighbor to the south, was not an area he could remember precisely having ventured into before, though as a boy he certainly must have. The cedar closed in as he moved, low and tight, and he caught only flashes now and again of the stark white rocks along the side of the draw. He could not imagine why he was there, an aging man at a child's game of exploring, fighting off the grasping limbs of cedars, at times having to drop on all fours and crawl along a trail pulverized by hoofprints left by horned and hairy creatures the night before, the air pungent with the smell of urine and manure.

He spooked a whitetail from his morning rest. The deer broke from a slight depression in a clump of cedars to his left, crashing through thick limbs, antlers clattering, presenting so brief a target of grayish brown that even had he been armed, he would not have been able to shoot. He shoved through tightly woven branches until he found the spot, spongy with decayed needles and still warm from the deer's body. When he scooped up and and sniffed a handful of rich humus from the depression, a riot of rotting needles and leaves from a small pinoak snuggled among the cedars, he found a piece of blackened bone, a little bone—he had no idea what kind—so he laid it aside and, intrigued, began skimming off layers of leafmold. The day was young yet and he was like a boy away from school and chores.

Soon he had cleared a spot of dark earth the size of a bath towel. Judging from the blackened stones and chunks of wood char and bone, someone had had a fire there at one time and cooked a large animal. As he unearthed the bones, he laid them out on smooth cedar-fall carpet behind him—none was indentifiable as part of any animal he was familiar with, but they were very old and charred. Then his fingers, running just beneath the crust of soil, found something large and round and smooth—simply a stone he thought at first, until he dug about it and lifted and felt its heft, and when he had brushed it free of soil he found staring from his hand the deep cold sockets of a fragile human skull, badly burned and lacking the lower jaw. Long he stared back, uncertain what to do, whether to return the skull and its attendant bones to their ancient burial bed or keep the find. A light wind was playing up from the south, and far off in the valley he could hear the sounds of dogs yapping and a woman calling a child.

He laid the skull behind him with the other

bones and resumed his excavation, eager now to discover what else the cache might yield. He scooped the soft earth away in small handfuls, allowing the soil to filter through his fingers onto the ground beside him.

"What'd you take with you, Chief?" he softly asked the bones behind him. "Gold or beads or guns? What?" But he knew that whatever he found would have to have withstood the intense flame that burned away all the man's smaller bones, ribs and fingers and toes, leaving the skull egg-shell thin, almost to the point of crumbling in his hands. At length he found half of the lower jaw, a mere sliver with two teeth imbedded in it, and more large bones, which he laid with the others.

He slowly ran his hands through the dirt, working in circles and going less than a quarter of an inch deep each time, filtering the fine soil through his fingers, flicking away nuggets of char and small stones that had no decided shape to them. Just as he was ready to believe that there were only bones, that the man was sent to his final rest with nothing to accompany him on that long, silent journey, his fingers closed on a little clump of something that felt different, grouped, as if placed there deliberately, and he withdrew a palmful of arrowheads and beads that at one time must have been wrapped or bagged in several layers of leather, remaining tightly bound as the bier collapsed and the leather burned away.

There were four perfectly formed arrowheads and an assortment of beads with holes made by a tiny auger, two small cylindrical stones, whose shapes meant nothing to him, and four large fangs that he surmised came from a predator. He blew and brushed away the dirt from his find and pocketed the small treasure, then returned with fervor to his digging.

But he found nothing more after nearly an hour of scraping away one thin layer of soil at a time, so he replaced the bones and pulled the earth back into the depression and sprinkled leaves over it until the spot looked almost the way he had found it. He wrapped the little treasure in his handkerchief and carried it back to the house, where he hid it in one of the storage sheds.

"Kiowa," he said softly as he entered the fragrant house, "it must have been a Kiowa chief who died here in the valley and they burned his body on the hill." How noble a way for the body to go, how wonderfully natural: the white-hot fire of rich cedar searing off that mortal shell, leaving the spirit of the Indian riding the winds, his ashes settling softly over the hills and valley he must have loved. He smiled and walked into the kitchen and with a finger tasted the brown gravy his wife was stirring in a pan.

He said nothing to the others. They would merely scoff, as they always had, at anything he brought down from the hills. His wife and children always called ridiculous his notions that Indians once camped along the valley, so one day he drove in to the Junction library and brought back books that established the fact that Comanches and Kiowas and Lipan Apaches had ranged in the area for hundreds of years. He laid the books out on the kitchen table and had them sit down and pass the books around.

"Now look where I've marked. They were *too* out here, all over the place, right here in this valley. Camped all up and down the river and up in the hills."

Lehman, the older son, glared at him. "So what? If they were here, so *what*? They were filthy beasts, and all they did was slay innocent white people and take women and children."

"Why do you persist in glorifying those savages?" his wife asked.

"Yeah," the younger son said, "they were heathen, filthy, disease-ridden, superstitious, brutal—you name anything bad and they were it." The boy was only thirteen at the time, bright as they come, but he was at an age when boys ought to believe in the nobility of Indians. "And you have never pronounced their name right. You say Kio-*way*, as in *neighbor* and *weigh*."

"Daddy," the daughter said, a mere switch of a thing, "you are not supposed to mark in those books—they are not ours."

"Just a Goddamned minute." He brought his hand hard down on the kitchen table where they were sitting. "I'll pronounce Kio-way *any* way I want to. But why do you call them heathen? Because they worshipped gods that didn't look like them? They worshipped the sun and moon and land and wind and water and—they worshipped what they saw and lived with and loved. They were in harmony with their world. And *naw*, they didn't have a Jesus with auburn hair and blue eyes that spoke modern English, which we never had neither but are too stupid to know or too proud to admit. Superstitious, yes, but no more than you are."

His eyes swept round the table. "You believe in prayer and divine intervention, with God coming down and helping out your football team on Friday nights, and wafers and wine and all that stuff, and none of you fail to mention it when a black cat crosses your path or when you see a single buzzard in the sky, and I never went to a cemetery with any of you in my entire life but what you got real quiet and serious and walked like you were walking on egg shells, like you were afraid you were going to wake some of them up! Sure, Indians killed and burned and destroyed people's houses and barns, but what they did they did because their culture allowed for it and because they figured that this land had been their since the beginning, which is more than can be said for the savages that kill and mug and rape people and destroy property in downtown Houston."

If he had shown them the cache he'd found and mentioned the bones, they'd proably say it was just some wetback that got drunk and rolled over into his fire and burned up. So he said nothing and went to the bathroom to wash up for dinner.

Though in his late fifties then, he was strong, tall and lean and vigorous of health, with no more thought of decline and death than he might have had as a boy in summer whiling away a long sun in the hills. Arguing with them was the most wearisome thing he'd ever done, and he never walked away from a confrontation feeling good or triumphant, no matter how right he might have been.

Now his body was failing fast and the present confrontation was probably the last one he would have with them. And this one he had to win. Their voices had died away, and he heard his sons getting into their cars and leaving. The house settled into late evening silence. The daughter shuffled down the hallway, stopped outside his door, then shuffled off again. He lay staring at the dark ceiling a long time, the only sounds that of cars passing along the street and dogs barking somewhere a few blocks over. An owl hooted in one of the neighbor's trees. An owl. Here in the city. He couldn't remember hearing an owl there before. Maybe it was a sign. But before he could decide what sort of sign it might be, sleep bore him away.

Awake long before dawn, he rose and quietly

made his way to the bathroom, where he kneeled and peed along the side of the bowl, making no sound at all, then stood unsteadily and rinsed his face with cold water. The tiles beneath his feet were as cold as the slab of a grave. Only the thickness of the tiles and four inches of concrete separated him from the earth that pulled at him, a strange mixture of red and gray clay hauled in from God knew where and packed by a yellow machine, layered and layered until the builders were certain bayou waters could never reach the house that would stand there. "Even the dirt's not real here," he told his daughter as they had stood watching one of the trucks dump its load.

Back in the dark bedroom he dressed in his old jeans and sweatshirt and field jacket and sat down on the bed and pulled on his boots. Now the mere act of tying them, so common to a boy of five, he found a heavy, fumbling business, even in the light, as if he were watching someone else's hands at work, the way a man of the soil finds threading a needle. In frustration he finally tied them in double knots and stood. "Keys," he said softly, "knife, billfold, checkbook," slipping his things into pockets as he inventoried.

He was almost to the kitchen when he heard his daughter whisper, "Daddy, where are you going this early?"

He continued into the kitchen and flipped on the coffee pot, whose small green eye was watching for six o'clock. It began to hiss and rumble.

"I decided I'm going out to the place for a few days. Got to tidy up some. I was going to try to get off without waking you up."

"Now, how do you intend to get there?" She came in and turned on the light above the stove. "I'll declare—you look like a tramp." She smiled and walked over and hugged him. "Just how in the world do you intend to go?"

"Bus," he said. "I was going to call a taxi, and then take the bus on out. There's one that leaves at eight o'clock. It'll get me there late today." The stove light cast his shadow, tall and gaunt, against the opposite wall.

"Daddy, you're sick. You're in no condition to travel. Why don't you have a cup of coffee and I'll fix you some breakfast and you go on back to bed. I'll talk to Lehman and Jimmy about driving you out this weekend for a look around. OK? If there's anything to be done, they can help. It might be nice to go out for awhile." She smiled prettily and poured his coffee, though the little stream was still trickling into the pot. Sometimes she looked exactly like her mother—slender and blond, her face beautiful even without makeup, even in the morning, when women's faces were supposed to look puffy and old.

He sat down at the table and blew across his cup. "Well, I thought I'd make this one myself. It'll probably be the last time I'll be able to do it."

"You might not can do it now," she said. "If they don't want to go, you and me and the kids'll go. This very weekend. I promise. And you can decide what needs to be done and Jimmy and Lehman will go out and do it. I'll shame'm into it."

He shook his head and sipped from his cup. "No. I think I'd like to go at least one more time by myself. I feel strong enough for the trip. I can sleep on the bus. Rest up. I'll take my medicine with me. Just want to mess around a little, tidy up. Won't do nothin' heavy, I promise."

"Daddy, this scares me. I want you here, where I can watch after you. It's been months since you were out there and that pump might act up again and you won't have water."

"If it does, I'll call somebody. I can always call

Silsbee. I'll be fine. Everything'll work. There's still water jugs in the refrigerator and two or three six-packs of beer. And that river's purer than that damned Ozarka you buy."

She smiled and patted him on the arm. "I got beer right here."

"Reckon I better go on out. May be the last time by myself."

She slumped in her chair. "OK. But I'm not going to say anything to Lehman and Jimmy about it as long as I can. Maybe you'll get back before they know. If you *get* back. They'll raise hell with me for letting you go." She stood and took a cell phone from its charger on the counter. "But you take this with you so that you can get help if you need it. Carry it everywhere you go, but don't turn it on until you call so that you don't run the battery down. I'll fix a little bag of cheese and crackers and fruit and stuff for you to snack on. Is there enough canned stuff for you to eat?"

"Yes'm, plenty. Pantry's full. Spam, chili, beans. Got   plenty of stuff out there." He slipped the little phone into his jacket pocket.

"I'll call a cab for you. You watch for him so he doesn't blow the horn and wake up the kids. And you remember to give me a call when you get out there, let me know you're OK."

"Yes'm."

Somewhere beyond San Antonio he woke from a series of short, fitful naps to a breathless awareness of a spiritual presence that the bus was moving through. It wrapped about him like a shawl, tighter and tighter, encompassing even his face until it was only with great difficulty that he managed to get any air at all. He thought briefly of his medicine, then drew his legs up into the seat and watched the vast land slide by, while the spirit hovered and enveloped and pursued.

"There's no permanence in any of it," he said to the piece of glass that separated him from the zipping landscape. "Nothing on this side." He breathed against the cool window and with his finger made a cross in the circle of fog. "Just what's out there."

He tried to think of death again, how it would come and when, but the spirit squeezed his chest, wrapped like cottony vapor about his face, and, panting like a puppy, he wanted only to be off the bus.

At the Segovia Truck Stop the driver pulled in for a cup of coffee and a break for the passengers and the old man got off, the spirit still wound tightly about him. He leaned against the front of the building, barely able to breathe, and tried calling a neighbor with the cell phone, but his fingers kept fumbling over the buttons.

"Goddamn it," he panted. He switched the little phone off and stuck it in his pocket and fed a quarter into the slot of a pay phone, leaned close and jabbed the numbers, spoke softly with someone, then sat on a bench waiting for his ride.

When after a few long minutes he saw an old blue truck boiling down the dirt road from the east, he took the two vials of medicine from his jacket pocket, studied them a few seconds, and dumped the contents into a garbage can, shuffling the can until the pills settled to the bottom.

The truck snorted up and stopped. The driver leaned and opened the door for him. "How you been, Mr. Turner?" He stuck out his hand and helped him in. It was one of Dan Silsbee's hired men—late thirties, lean and leathery from West Texas sun and wind. His hand felt hard and strong as steel. Turner had known him for years.

"Well, Bobby, you can see, can't you?" His

voice was weak and came with great effort. "Weigh about half what I did, got the color of a catfish belly, weak as a Goddamned baby."

"You look fine to me."

"Better get your eyes checked, boy."

"You get you somethin' t'eat yet?"

"Naw, I'm not hungry. Just take me on to the ranch. I'll get something there."

"Yessir."

The truck left the smooth pavement of the truck stop apron and rattled onto caliche. The dust it had left coming in was still hanging dead-wind.

"Mr. Silsbee was s'prised they let you come out by yourself."

The old man raised his voice over the rattling of the truck. "*Let* me? They didn't have any *say* in it. I can still do on my own." He looked off across the valley. "Sonsabitches."

"Well, Mr. Silsbee always said you was tough as limestone. You'll probably be comin' out here when I'm too old to drive down to get you. Guess I'll have to get one of my boys to do it."

The old man tried to laugh, but the pressure was still on his chest and face. It might have been the dust or the glare, but he could barely make out the features of the man behind the wheel. He seemed to be weaving in and out of fog.

"Anything special bring you out, Mr. Turner? My boys—"

"Naw, naw, just cleaning up some is all. Tell Dan that I'm gon' burn those old brushpiles up in the hills, tomorrow probably, not to get concerned if he sees smoke up there. They ought to be good and dry by now. Been adding to'm ever time I come out. Big stacks. It's about time I burned'm. Just something I need to get done, you know."

"You need any help?" the driver yelled over the

noise of the truck on loose caliche. "You look like you might could use a little help. I'll send one of the boys up. My oldest one's nearly sixteen now, works like a horse. He's got his own chainsaw, and I'll let him use the truck if you need it. You can give him three or four dollars a hour—hell, *two*—and he'll be happy."

The old man shook his head. "Naw," he yelled back, the best he could, "I appreciate it, but there's not much to it. Just need a match put to'm. You remember, you and a couple of wetbacks helped me up there a couple of years ago. Those big ol' stacks up on Hill One? I just got to burn'm. I saw on the weather report that y'all got some rain through here a couple of days ago, and I can tell by the ditches that you did, so there shouldn't be any danger of the fire gettin' loose. Gon' clean up a little bit on the top of that hill. Not gon' be out here but a couple of days. Gotta tidy up some, in case it's my last trip out."

"Aw, like I say, you'll be comin' after I'm dead and gone and I ain't even forty. Just call me if you need some help. And call me when you get ready to go back."

The old man nodded and they drove on without speaking until the truck stopped at the gate of the property and he got out and shook the driver's hand. Dust billowed over him.

"You sure you're OK, Mr. Turner? Your color ain't good."

He waved him on. "It's just the dust. Makes everything look pale. I'm fine. I'll be fine. I got to—"

"You got you something t'eat in the house?" He motioned to the little bag the old man was carrying. "Can't have much groceries with you there."

"Got some crackers and things in this bag.

Got all kinds of stuff in the house. Main thing is, I got beer in the refrigerator. I'll get by."

"Beer's all *I'd* want. You don't need no milk or—"

"Naw, I'll be fine." He waved and headed toward the house.

Even before he had reached the little split-rail fence that kept sheep away from the house the pressure of the spirit, whatever it was, had lifted, and by the time he finished a handful of cheese and crackers and a beer before the great stone fireplace he felt like a much younger man. He flipped the bottle into the plastic trash can by the door and went to the refrigerator for another.

"I can do without milk, but I got to have beer," he said to the glassy eyes of the animals that looked down on him. He tried to keep a case of Corona in the refrigerator all year round.

After he'd finished his beer he tried to dial his daughter on the cell phone, but again his fingers seemed too large and awkward for the tiny keys, so he turned it off and laid it on the kitchen counter and called her on the old beige phone on the kitchen counter. He liked the way his fingers felt spinning the little dial, he liked the way it worked, he liked the sound.

The call finished, he ate a can of sardines on the screened-in porch off the kitchen and drank some water from a jug he'd taken from the refrigerator. Then he lit a cigar and smoked it halfway though before he rose to his feet and ventured out into the yard. Off to the south he could hear someone yelling for cows.

He sat a long time smoking and drinking beer, watching the sun settle down over the hills across the valley, leaving his own in purple shadow while the peaks of those beyond which it set were bathed in a golden glory, sanctified, holy. As dark descended, he thought briefly about walking to the top of Hill One and checking out the piles, but he wasn't sure he had the strength, so he pulled a lawn chair out into the yard, set a six-pack of beer beside it, and watched the stars, focusing his mind on the incalculable dimensions of space. Four satellites and two shooting stars later, he went in and undressed.

For hours he kept vigil against the dark that he dreaded and welcomed. He chose the couch before the fireplace instead of his bed, and though it was not a particularly cool April night and the heat of the sun still radiated from the block walls, he built a roaring fire and kept it stoked and fed throughout the evening and into the morning hours. The flames threw amorphous shadows all about the room and returned to him as tiny points of lights in the glass eyes of the creatures that stared silent from the walls.

Beer after beer he watched the flames rise and engulf the fresh logs he fed on, watched them consume and purify until all that was left was a jumble of twinkling embers, whereupon he stood unsteadily and slid onto the iron cradle a new log from the big wooden box by the hearth. In minutes the heat from beneath ignited the log, fine flames wrapped about it, and the room danced with shadows again.

All night long he watched, fed his fire and drank, looking from one hanging face to the next, their eyes sparkling and flashing then fading to a dull glow then flashing again as the fire rose and fell.

I've got to take the Indian's stuff back up there. Gotta put it back. Nobody else'll know what it is. Need to check on Daddy's grave. Then burn the brushpiles, tidy up. Get things in order. Won't get another chance. Notions in and out of his head all night long. So much to do. Not even time to sleep.

But sleep he did, sometime in the early morning.

At dawn he crawled from the couch and stirred the gray-white ashes, added kindling, coaxed the fire back, laid on a single log. He drank a glass of water, ate some cheese and crackers, and stumbled to the bathroom and washed his face, then dressed, checked to see that his snake pistol was loaded, and stuck a lighter in his pocket.

In one of the outbuildings he climbed onto a stepladder and shoved his hand up among the rafters and took down the little bundle of stones he had taken from the Indian's grave and slipped them into his pocket. He picked up a large red metal can, shook it, and hoisted it onto his shoulder and started off across the mesquite thicket that lay between him and Hill One. The morning was young yet, the sun just beginning to glaze the tips of the trees on the ridge, where he knew in another few minutes it would thrust up and throw its first fingers of light across the valley and onto the hills on the other side. He loved to watch it happen, the way the light would begin high on the hills and slide slowly down as the purple of night drained away out of the river bottom like sacramental wine until the whole valley shone bright in the sun.

The walk was a long one and tough up a narrow dirt road whose ruts over the winter had deepened, the mud hardened by the wind and sun into concrete castings and curled like frost heaves where the last truck went through—the sheepman's he presumed, but perhaps a hunter's. His shoulders wearied and he set the big can of diesel fuel down and picked it up by the handle, using its weight to propel his body forward, letting it strike the ground at the end of a stride, hoisting and slinging it forward again, so that the red can seemed to have a life of its own, hopping, the man fastened to it merely following where it led. Every hundred feet or so he would stop and sit on the can and rest, then pick it up with the other hand and resume his lurching stride.

Halfway up the path that led to the top of the hill, while he was resting on the can, his heart thrashing in its cage, he heard the outside phone bell at the house. His daughter was calling to check on him. In half an hour she would call again. But by then he would be on top of the hill and beyond the sound of the bell. He rose unsteadily and continued up the road. Far ahead, in the still gloom of morning, he could see the foot of the hill path where its white rock fanned out into the grass of the draw.

Half carrying the can now, half dragging, he managed it up the tortuous path that wound through low cedars around the edge of the hill. Below he could see the jumble of white rock that lined the draw. When he had achieved the summit, he followed a path soft with needles of cedar until he broke into a clearing and reached the first of the pyramids of brush and limbs. It sat in an opening between two stands of heavy cedar and pinoak. There he stopped and rested again until his heart quieted and his strength rallied, then he unscrewed the can and poured perhaps half a gallon of diesel along the edge of the pile, touched his lighter to it, and watched as the flame broke red and lovely and a roil of black smoke rose above the stack in a slight drift on the morning sky. He stood a while before the blazing pile, backing off as heat pressed against his face and arms.

"One down," he said softly.

Farther on, in a wide rocky opening, he lit another pile. Behind him he could hear the crackling and popping of the first pile. When he turned to look, a black mushroomed cloud towered and flames leapt in rapacious tongues above the line of low trees that separated him from it. The second pile caught readily and he moved on, half carrying, half dragging the can of fuel.

"Two." His breath was ragged and shallow.

He passed around a clump of cedars and across another opening where a small stack of limbs squatted, not worth his time, on through a little patch of pinoaks into yet another clearing, in whose center a pile of dead cedar loomed higher than the peak of his house, wide at the base and tapering slowly, the limbs and logs thickly laced. He remembered well when they built it, joking all the while about how if they kept on, it might rank as one of the ten Wonders of the World. It took them almost two full days.

In sight of the cedar thicket where the old Indian's grave lay, he set the can down and rested a long time before moving again, summoning whatever strength remained for this last and greatest mound. He studied the cedar thicket but could not remember where to enter to find the grave, could not even decide whether he wanted to. In time his heart quieted and his breath deepened as he turned from the cedars and faced the pyramid of gray limbs that towered against the sky.

"Need to put his stuff back," he said to himself. "Need to put it back."

He lifted the heavy can and sloshed fuel all around the periphery, letting it dribble down across limbs and logs, then set the can aside and fished out his lighter, flared it, and leaned toward the oil-dark base. He stood back and studied the pyramid again. It seemed like a stairway deep into the sky, the way it narrowed to its peak, the logs like steps he might climb. He snuffed the lighter.

The old man took the Indian's clutch of treasure from his pocket and spread it in his open hand, noting how after all the heat that they had gone through, the stones and arrowheads and beads still held their color in the rising sun, the fangs still shone white. He looked once again toward the cedar thicket and pushed the bundle back into his pocket. Checking the can to see how much diesel remained, he lifted it and wedged it in the branches as high as he could reach, then carefully began to climb the stack, pushing the can higher as he climbed.

His body seemed no longer to belong to him, slave to some vast, mysterious energy that purged him of pain and pulled him higher and higher until, scratched and almost without breath, he achieved the top, concave with matted branches and cedar needles like a cradle. He sat a very long time and rested. To someone watching from the edge of the cedars he would have looked like some sort of ancient nesting bird, his white-feathered head emblazoned with sun against the shocking blue of the sky.

Far off across the shimmering ocean of cedar and stunted oaks lay the valley floor, half of it purple and hazy, half in sun. Columns of smoke still rose from the first fires, no longer angry and black now but graying, mellowing, the diesel and heavy pitch having burned away, and he knew that what was left was no more than a collapsing bed of bright coals and log ends and ashes. In a few hours there would be only a warm gray circle where the pile had been.

He looked toward the cedar thicket. "Time to ride the wind, Chief. Got your stuff with me. It's back on the hill." He uncapped the can and poured fuel oil all around and beneath him, drizzling it through logs and limbs and clumps of needle, dumping what remained over his clothes. Then the empty red can tumbled away down the slope of the pyramid like a child's toy, bouncing and skittering, coming to rest finally beside a slab of stone.

From the nest of cedar limbs beneath him the old man selected a branch with a clutch of needles damp with oil and removed from his jacket pocket the lighter, spun the little wheel, then held the flame out to the limb. It flared, and he flung it out and down toward the base of the stack, where the brown needles of the lower branches caught up the fire and fed it and the oil-dark jumble of cedar above ignited and he could smell the sulphur of diesel fuel and hear the crackling fire, feel the press of heat from beneath as a column of black smoke rolled over him. With his left hand he clutched the little leather bundle in his pocket and with the right pulled his pistol from its holster, cocked it, and lay back. He stared straight into the darkening sun.

Late that morning Dan Silsbee was scattering range cubes among his milling cows when he heard the dull report of a gun from the top one of Turner's hills, but he knew the old man was on the place, and the shot was of no consequence to him, no more than the new billow of smoke. Turner was burning brush, and judging by the way the red flames leapt above the trees in angry, ragged sheets, this third pile was a big one. When he glanced over his shoulder on the way back to the barn, the column of smoke had risen straight up, at its tip curling into a tight dark fist. Silsbee stood and watched the fist loosen as the column toppled and faded from black to gray, then almost silver, drifting out over the hills and valley toward the river, settling gently like a spirit coming home.